I0517322

Illustrators:
Marge Simon: pages 8, 31, 68, and 76
Baishampayan Seal: page 21
Chris Friend: pages 29, 65, and 73
Sandy DeLuca: front and back covers, and pages 3, 19, 40, and 86
Elizabeth Hattie Pierce-Collins: pages 4, 11, 44, and 80
Denny E. Marshall: pages 25 and 56
James Masters: pages 51 and 90

Night to Dawn No. 39, April, 2021, Copyright 2021 by Barbara Custer. All rights revert to individual author and artist after publication. ISSN # 1542-1430; ISBN: 978-1-937769-67-3
Night to Dawn is a semi-annual publication of fiction, poetry, artwork, articles, and review.
Orders, editorial, and queries: Barbara Custer, P. O. Box 643, Abington, PA 19001
Email: barbaracuster@hotmail.com or ntdsubmissions@gmail.com
PayPal orders: venus1021@juno.com.
Submissions: ntdsubmissions@gmail.com; Web: www.bloodredshadow.com

Pickings and Tidbits

Top of the balloon to ya'll! ☺

We're coming off a severe winter. In the meantime, the apocalypse of the movie screen and the printed page has become a reality. Like most people, I carry a mask and sanitizer along with my wallet. Kevin R. Doyle's "Who Is?" portrays a microbe that makes Corona seem like the common cold and threatens humanity. Is such a microbe possible? I wonder. Hopefully, by this printing, the vaccine will be available to inoculate people against Corona. In the meantime, please be careful and stay safe.

For *Night to Dawn 39*, I'd like to introduce a new artist, Baishampayan Seal. His poem "Beneath the Moonshine" and illustration appear on pages 20 and 21. Sandy DeLuca did the front and back covers for this issue, along with interior art. She also did the front cover for NTD 38; her granddaughter Gianna inspired that art. Marge Simon has two more excerpts, "Raw Liver" and "Sleepless Nights," from *The Demeter Diaries*, poetry, and a flash piece, "Ivan and Goddess of Time," along with accompanying art. *The Demeter Diaries* was an excellent book, and I strongly recommend giving it a read. James Masters, Denny E. Marshall, Elizabeth Hattie Pierce, and Chris Friend also have illustrations here. Next issue, James Fay will make a comeback with his poetry and an illustration.

My intern, Keily Blair, edited some of the tales in this issue. She's been a jewel of a worker, and I'm glad to have her on board. Her fiction, "Communion," appears in this issue, and no, it doesn't involve wafers, but a mirror that, shall I say, attracts blood.

Lee Clark Zumpe's poetry and fiction continue to delight the reader. "The High Priest of Turmiz" features a city where innocents die to appease its young and hungry gods. "When Shadows Scream" struck close to my heart as the horrors take place in a nursing home. A physician there feeds the shadows of the hapless residents to a demon. In "Two Winters," Zumpe describes grisly killings through the narrator's eyes. I thought the narrator was a witness, but he isn't—quite. In "The Great Hall of Ahkurst," an elderly man lives with his own kind in an underground city that falls to ruins. Grieving the loss of what was once a thriving city, he huddles in a room with his peers, anticipating death.

Margaret L. Carter's back with "Support Group," featuring Dr. Roger Darvell, one of my favorite characters. He and his wife are protagonists in *Dark Changeling* and *Child of Twilight*, both excellent books. Both books have been combined into a Kindle edition titled *Twilight's Changelings*, and I recommend reading. Hal Kempka's back with "Milkweed," which opens with a lonely man looking for a date. She introduces him to butterflies, but not the nice kind.

Matthew Wilson wrote an intriguing flash piece, "I Am No Witch," plus several delightful poems. Linda Barrett's "Lianne" features a detective who is a canine-human mutant. She searches for Lianne, a missing vestal, but some people don't want to be found. Rajeev Bhargava's "Brass Mineral Lighthouse for Terminally Undead" touches on the pandemic but in a roundabout way. Instead of humans getting sick, monsters are, and Rajeev's tale includes all kinds. Christopher Dabrowski's "Simon Wallow" is a time-travel piece, but with enough horror to fit into NTD. During a trip to the Cretaceous period, a crewmember's pet swallows escapes, passing on their genetic modifications to the existing birds of that time with disastrous results. And if you're looking for human monsters and ferocious crocodiles, you'll find them in Todd Hanks' "The Crocodile Pit."

Rod Marsden's tale, "Hearts Rule," gives the reader a look into the cruel, futuristic society which serves as a setting for his book, *50 Dragons*. Keily has helped with editing the sequel, *Dragon Queen*. I'm hoping to release it before spring.

This past year, I had the pleasure of taking Kathryn Craft's *Your Novel Year* mentorship. For some time, I've had Walter Mitty dreams of taking a writing course like this. Life got in the way for many years, but I was able to do this in 2020. Because she spends a lot of time critiquing and mentoring each student, she rarely takes more than six per mentorship. Three students, including myself, took the class, but because of Corona, we did most of our lessons on Zoom, and then later, WebEx. I'd gotten stuck writing my sequel to *When Blood Reigns*, and taking Kathryn Craft's course opened my eyes to what I've been doing wrong. First up, I wrote my first chapter from the villain's point of view. Bad idea because the reader will assume that the point of view character in the first chapter is the protagonist. What's more, I had two protagonists, Alexis from the first two books, and Maddie, a new character.

Maddie stole the show, but you can only have one protagonist. And Maddie's got a host of weaknesses, so I've got my revising cut out for me. A good protagonist can have problems, but he or she must be a fighter and establish their agency. There's homework—it keeps you focused on your work and trains you to work under deadlines. You can check out Kathryn's books and information for writers on www.kathryncraft.com.

With that, gentle reader, I shall send you to "The High Priest of Turmiz," the first of many treats you'll find in NTD 39. I hope you enjoy them as much as I've enjoyed serving them. ~ *Barbara* 😊 😊

The High Priest of Turmiz
by
Lee Clark Zumpe

Deep in the Northern Mountains in the city called Turmiz, the altar upon which the necromancer Ak Khun Khan shed the blood of innocents to appease the young and hungry gods still stands enshrouded by hoary shadows.

Though few would venturento the subterranean corridors which lead to the Old One's sacred temple, the Priesthood maintains an access point through which pilgrims wishing to make an offering may pass. In those tunnels beneath that highland sanctuary, slinking through dismal and abandoned burrows, it is rumored that the raspy voice of the long-interred High Priest echoes down the ages, whispering invocations.

Turmiz, the city purportedly built by dragonkind before men conquered these lands, is hard-featured and terrible to behold. Tall, black, windowless towers stab skyward. The city walls are ominous and impenetrable, and the city itself seems to intimate that it is both as old and as undying as the mountains surrounding it. At first sight, it appears that the rock vomited up this geometric monstrosity and that men simply infest its honeycomb caverns.

The Scroll of Zahkmuur tells that Ak Khun Khan first stumbled upon this place in the Dark Ages before Amoroz disbanded the Sect of the Black Goat. In those ancient days, the gods still attended this divine highland, walked upon the consecrated ground of the Plateau of Uddath Angk, and delivered their word directly unto the apostles. There was no need for divination or interpretation of omens, nor was there any distortion of the gods' will by ignorant and self-absorbed members of the Priesthood.

In the Year of the Blood Moon, Xamol first journeyed to Turmiz with a dozen and one black-hooded acolytes. The Great Reformer in his youth vowed to reveal the wicked underpinnings of the realm's heritage and – during the course of his career – promised to purge the Priesthood of all the depraved perversions of the Scripture that harkened back to the days of Ak Khun Khan. Xamol the Purifier came to Turmiz as a vigorous, strong-willed, fervent revolutionary, eager to challenge the arcane mystics who swore allegiance to the legacy of the Old One.

The followers of Ak Khun Khan's disciplines entertained Xamol's party and witnessed his exhortation on the malignancy of derivative dogma. In their lavish shrine set deep in the mountain, they gave ear to the Great Reformer as he admonished the assembly of Turmiz for deifying the image of the Old One, praising him in hymns, and making sacrifices in his name. Respectfully, they feasted with their presumptuous guests, shared ivory-yellow wine served in golden goblets, and even prayed together at the feet of the idol of Rahtu.

Yet, never once did the Priesthood of Turmiz yield to Xamol the Purifier's insistence that they renounce the name of Ak Khun Khan.

And so it was that Xamol, acting under the authority of the Yharim Dynasty and a vassal of the emperor, dismissed the acting High Priest of Turmiz and detained other high-ranking adherents of the Old One's teachings. Soldiers stood guard outside the grim and grand temples to ensure that improper worship could not take place, and all known entrances to the network of tunnels beneath the city were either sealed or secured. Xamol even ordered the city guard to confiscate religious icons related to the worship of the Old One, and popular fetishes of Ak Khun Khan were collected from merchants and destroyed.

An inquisition convened, and Xamol selected a dozen and one errant priests to interview. These he assigned to his hooded acolytes with the instructions that all means be employed to secure from each an acknowledgment of iniquity and a detailed confession of the profane ceremonies relative to the blasphemous idolatry of Ak Khun Khan. The Great Reformer taught torture as a potent tool of persuasion, and his subordinates had grown adept in the unconventional techniques their master favored.

Appropriating the governor's palace, Xamol banished the nobles – whose support of the zealots in Turmiz was well-known – to the streets. A horde of commoners gathered to protest the persecution. In darkened chambers within the palace, the instruments of tortures were revealed one by one: Flesh-tearers, thumbscrews, shin-crushers, skull-crackers, three-thonged scourges, cudgels, and cords. All of these crept into the candlelight under the knowing hands of the ardent inquisitors. The mere sight of such atrocious contrivances had been known to break many a man's resolution, but the followers of Ak Khun Khan were dedicated to their faith.

For days, the corridors of that place were flooded with the wailings of the accused, and by night, their pitiful weeping spilled into the streets where their patrons huddled. Occasionally, the assemblage vented shuddering groans in sympathy.

On the fifth day of torture, the hooded acolytes of Xamol came before him to report the last of the priests had died under the inquisition. Not one had conceded indiscretions, confessed to abominations, or declared that the adoration of the Old One amounted to blasphemy. They stood silently, their faces obscured by their vestments, their expressions hidden from their master, as they awaited chastisement and direction.

Xamol, the Great Reformer, fumed. He considered apprehending another handful of priests but suspected that torture would prove ineffective on them as well. To crop this putrescent branch of worship, Xamol realized he would have to venture into the subterranean corridors and search out Ak Khun Khan's sacred temple deep in the heart of the mountain. Upon finding the repellent lair of the wretched Old One, he would oversee the destruction of all traces of this man's filthy existence.

Long after the black tide of night had drowned the high country in darkness, and the angry masses of the peasantry had taken their leave of the streets outside the palace to scurry back to their cave-like dwellings in the ancient city, Xamol and his company retired from the halls of the governor's residence and sped to a secluded passage under strict guard. They marched past a dozen sacrificial stones, glancing at dragontail wisps of incense dancing in the torchlight. They sped down, through cobweb-draped channels where shadow seemed to hold sway and the icy air bit at exposed flesh unceasingly. They passed beyond the cryptic pictographs of the prehistoric mountain clans and further still until the cave had dwindled into a narrow shaft and the floor threatened to meet the ceiling.

Xamol pushed onward on his hands and knees, certain his persistence would prove meritorious.

Then, finally, the constricted crawlway opened into a vast chamber. Xamol's torch burned a patch of comfortless illumination into the primeval gloom. Its flickering flames begot twisting shadows which alluded to faceless horrors just outside the circle of light. He froze at the sight before him. At the center of the room, the infamous altar stood waiting – the Old One's own book of profane writings silently anticipating the rebirth of its application. A thousand dormant candles encircled the place, and as the Great Reformer moved forward, he wordlessly implored his followers to use their torches to light the candles.

He alone approached the altar. His fingers drifted hesitantly across the text for a moment; then he drew back fearfully as though touching the words might make him believe. Yet, once his gaze fell upon the lines he could not turn away, and as he read the ancient verses, he could hear Ak Khun Khan's voice murmur in his head.

Finally, Xamol wrenched himself free from the accursed tome. The candles now burned brightly, and the extent of the chamber was revealed. In every corner, there loomed the face of a dragon, gaping maws ringed by grisly fangs, hideous talons clenched, narrow eyes glaring. The Great Reformer shivered at the fearsome renderings in stone, even though he knew them to be nothing more than sculptures.

These were Ak Khun Khan's gods – the false gods of Turmiz. The Old One taught that men are little more than pawns to the descendants of the dragonkind, and that someday their kin would rise again from secreted caverns to lord over the kingdoms forged by the lesser race. The Priesthood of Turmiz echoed his beliefs in their sermons, and the people of Turmiz had been corrupted by these lies.

No longer could such defilement of the truth be allowed. Xamol the Purifier would not permit it.

"Burn the book," the Great Reformer said, turning to his acolytes, "and return with hammers to deface these awful icons. Nevermore shall the people of Turmiz speak of the dragonkind!"

He awaited the execution of his orders but found his subordinates unmoving. He repeated his mandate, shaking his fists and cursing the spirit of Ak Khun Khan with considerable passion. Still, the hooded acolytes stood motionless as though his words had not reached them.

Then, one by one, they drew back their hoods and revealed their faces. Xamol staggered backwards as he gazed upon the scaly green flesh of a dozen and one descendant of the dragonkind. His heart raced as their serpent-eyes regarded him, and he whimpered as they encircled him. When their grisly fangs bore down on him and their hideous talons raked his flesh, his screams echoed through the subterranean corridors and rang out through the streets.

And after a moment, all was quiet again in the city called Turmiz.

The End

Vampire Jack by Marge Simon

Bold as a crow on road kill,
nothing phases him, not even
the fancy ladies of the night.

He's beyond the scope,
hat a-tilt, scarf stained
with scarlet drops that soon
will dry to match his shirt.

No man like our Jack,
but then, he's got stuff going
for him—things we don't want
to know about that smile
half-formed, around those
handsome lips, swollen
with the blood of
sweet young things.

Milkweed
by
Hal Kempka

Walter's mother had always disapproved of him having any type of relationship with a woman. He ignored her, but his awkward, inexperienced approach usually scared women off. After she died, he joined an online dating service, figuring if a woman got to know him before they met, all would be well.

The initial responses to his profile appeared promising, and he made contact with several women. Although they lived miles away, he felt proud of his ability to establish a rapport. He sought to meet them, but they countered with numerous excuses.

Walter grew tired of the rejection and decided to try one last club before giving up. A week after joining, he received an introduction email from a young woman. She said she read his profile and felt that they might have a lot in common.

"I am a lonely, attractive, professional woman," she said, "and am seeking an independent, considerate man I can wrap my arms around and love. I am not into games and have no interest in someone with other attachments."

She gave her name as Lily and enclosed a picture along with her personal email rather than her dating club address. In her picture, Lily appeared to be on a ladder rung somewhere between homely and beautiful, enough on the latter side for Walter to consider the possibilities.

He emailed her back but gave up when several days passed, and she had not replied. One afternoon, he found her response in his inbox. Lily lived an hour away and wanted to meet for coffee. If either felt uncomfortable, she said, they would leave. No harm and no foul.

Walter replied and arranged the date. He recognized her immediately because she looked no different than her picture.

"Walter?" she asked as he approached.

"You must be Lily," he replied and shook her hand.

They stood at the counter and ordered their lattes the same way. He caught himself leaning in to smell her hair, which carried a faint floral aroma. He carried their coffee to a secluded table, where they divulged their respective likes, dislikes, and common interests.

She enjoyed the outdoors and exercised regularly at a health club, and he was a jogger. She made wine as a hobby, and he brewed homemade beer. Walter finally asked what it was she was looking for in a man.

"I joined the club," she said, "because I felt like a caterpillar desiring to be transformed into a butterfly. All I want is for a man to love me and make me feel beautiful. Too many people want to play games, and I have found that so disappointing."

At that moment, Walter knew he wanted her. He hoped, however, the feeling would be mutual, and he did not want to screw it up. He planned to do whatever it took to make her feel beautiful.

As the evening progressed, neither suggested a lack of interest. When the coffee shop closed, he offered to drive her home. Lily accepted and gave him directions to her place, which was a quaint bungalow that snuggled up to the wooded area of a local park.

Before getting into the car, she leaned toward him and placed her head against his cheek. Walter shivered as her eyelashes batted against his cheek.

"Know what that is?" she asked, with a suggestive lilt in her voice. "It's a butterfly kiss. Butterflies do that to flowers before they collect pollen."

He could barely contain himself while they drove to her place. Upon arriving, they sat in the car talking for several minutes.

Finally, Lily said, "I don't usually do this, but would you care to come in for a glass of wine? I have some fresh dandelion wine in the fridge."

"Absolutely," he replied.

He tingled with excitement, thinking about the possibilities. They stepped from the car and walked toward the house. Lily stopped and bent toward a small strip of clustered, pinkish-white flowers adorning the plants growing alongside the walkway. She held a cluster of the dainty flowers in her hand and motioned for him to lean toward them.

"Aren't they beautiful?" she asked and looped her arm through his. "They are milkweed, and butterflies just love them. Their aroma is so intoxicating it makes me tingle."

She snuggled up against him and led him into the house. Upon stepping inside, she surprised him with a passionate kiss on the lips.

Walter held her close and ran his hands from her waist at the small of her back up toward her shoulder blades. He could feel her ribs expand and contract in concert with her breathing. Lily wrapped her arms around his neck and pressed against him. Her hot breath emanated with the flowery aroma of the plants along the walkway.

"I want you so badly," she whispered.

Lily kissed him and slid her tongue between his lips. She dueled with his tongue and overpowered him with her passion. Walter opened his eyes and stared stunned as her nose and pulsating lips transformed into a proboscis-like appendage.

The proboscis flicked at his mouth, but before he could react. it slithered between his lips and down his throat. His face turned deep crimson, and he gagged. He fought to breathe while his stomach gurgled and bloated.

Lily's skin turned prickly, and Walter heard the distinct sound of material tearing apart. He pushed her away and glanced downward. Lily's torso turned waxy gray and lengthened. Her body then split apart, and blood splattered his shirt and trousers. Barbed, centipede-like legs sprouted through her skin and enveloped him.

Walter tried to fight her off, but her legs bound his arms and legs against his body. The last he saw was the look of terror on his face reflecting in each octagonal segment of her saucer-shaped, onyx eyes.

After sucking out his liquified internal organs, Lily dragged Walter's wrinkled shell of a corpse into the back yard. She placed him on a mulching pile of rotting corpses and returned to the house looping and stretching, slinky-like.

Sated and tired, Lily curled up in her cocoon-like bed to digest her meal. Walter would never know it, but he had made her feel like the butterfly she was on her way to becoming.

The End

A Lost Stranger by Matthew Wilson

Hateful witches dancing
Celebrating the arrival of death
Here comes the worst of kings
Hail our lord Macbeth.

Communion
by
Keily Blair

Dani stood before the covered mirror. One hand grasped a fistful of the sheet. She planned to count to three, but her lips couldn't even form "one." The hand holding the bloody hammer shook despite the deep breaths she took. Her bandaged arms ached.

In her mind's eye, she could see its silvery frame with the metal vines wrapped around it, the metal flowers blossoming on the corners. It was what drove Alicia to convince Dani to buy it for her, though they had little money. All of Alicia's treatments and the mirror was expensive.

Dani's grip on the hammer grew firm, still. Her eyes narrowed.

She drew the hammer back and removed the sheet.

****

"It looks gaudy," Dani said. "I don't know how I let you talk me into this."

Dani and Alicia stood in the room designated "Alicia's office" in their two-bedroom apartment. The mirror had arrived an hour before Dani had gotten home from work, and the sight of it made her stomach twist with nerves. It had cost nearly a whole paycheck, and now the permanent reminder of Alicia's tendency toward big spending would collect dust with the other reminders: a treadmill for when Alicia swore she'd exercise every day, a giant aquarium filled with exotic fish — fish that Dani now cared for — during Alicia's aquatics phase, expensive paintings piled up in a closet after Alicia no longer wanted to be an art collector, and now a full-length, ornamental mirror for Alicia to practice her self-affirmations. It was likely that she would use it for a day or two, and then it would end up forgotten.

"If I have to do it anyway," Alicia had said, "I want to do it in style."

Dani wished she had the heart to say "no." She used to say it all the time to Alicia's dangerously expensive whims, but it had grown more difficult. The purchases were the only things that still brought a spark of joy to Alicia's eyes. Dani wouldn't deny her that joy.

She gazed at her reflection in the antique mirror and grimaced. The bags under her eyes seemed more pronounced in the dim lighting. There was a scar on her upper lip from where she'd tripped and split it open when she was a kid. Her blonde hair was matted and oily. Her skin had broken out in several places, though she couldn't remember having a breakout past the age of seventeen. She had lost a button on her red blouse and hadn't even noticed. Her jeans were stained from a coke she'd spilled on herself days ago. Her gaze shifted to Alicia's reflection.

She didn't look nearly as bad as Alicia, but she'd never say that out loud. Alicia's self-esteem had taken enough hits since she had begun chemotherapy. Her pale yellow dress hung off of her emaciated frame since she'd refused to buy more clothing when she lost weight. Dani didn't know what to say when Alicia's beautiful, chestnut hair had begun to fall out. Dani had remained silent even as Alicia's pale skin darkened with purple bruises. Alicia's desire for the mirror had been an improvement. Maybe she would actually practice the self-affirmations the therapist had given her. The therapist had gone on and on about "positive body image in the wake of chemotherapy." Dani thought she was full of it, but Alicia had eaten up every word, and Dani would never crush Alicia's hopes to return to some sort of normalcy.

She'd been friends with Alicia ever since Dani's freshman year of high school. They'd started dating each other three years ago, right after Alicia had moved back into town after graduating from college. The attraction hadn't been anything extraordinary. Dani had simply matured through college experiences, and Alicia had left behind her fear of commitment somewhere along the way. There had been one night where Alicia had lingered after a party to play card games with Dani. Sometime around one in the morning, after a heated argument involving Alicia's bold turn, the cards lay forgotten as Dani tasted the peppermint on Alicia's lips.

Passion drove Alicia, and it was that passion that Dani had fallen for. Alicia was the type of woman to make an average walk through a local park seem like a hike along the Appalachian Trail. She would point out flower species and birds that Dani had never heard of, had never truly seen until Alicia had opened her eyes. She was the type of woman to make a bad amateur poetry night seem like a reading by a poet laureate. She would lean in close to Dani's ear, husky voice whispering her interpretation of the stumbling poet's shaky words, and she would paint skies and faraway lands that Dani could only see through the lens of her voice.

Once the initial fire and passion had cooled into a bond as strong as steel, they'd started talking marriage. They had only rented the apartment a few months ago, right before Alicia's diagnosis split their world open. She'd quit her job almost right after. Dani had promptly dropped out of college during her senior year to find a second job to pay for the mounting bills. Working two jobs wasn't an issue, though the mirror had taken a chunk out of her paycheck. Alicia's spending habits only seemed fueled by her declining condition, though it was Dani who would be paying back the credit card after all of this was over, one way or another.

One way or another. She didn't want to think about that. She'd only been to a funeral once, and it had been for some great-grandmother she'd barely known. The idea of Alicia, made-up in a coffin, dressed in her Sunday best—

"You look tired," Alicia said.

Dani pulled away from the mirror to kiss her head. She wasn't going to acknowledge the exhaustion, not to her.

"Come on, you need to eat," she said. "I'll make your favorite."

Alicia's expression made Dani's stomach twist in knots. Eating had been almost painful for her. Eating had become unpleasant for Dani as well, but she forced herself to eat in front of Alicia, even if her stomach was so twisted in knots that each bite nearly made her retch.

"Come on," she said. "You love lentil stew."

The best approach had been to pretend nothing was wrong, that the cancer wasn't rotting away the insides of her girlfriend. She reached for Alicia's hand, but Alicia recoiled.

"Sorry," she said. "I think I'll stay up here a while. Practice those affirmations."

Dani nodded. She left the room but waited outside the door, thankful for the carpet that always hid her steps. Alicia said nothing at first, but then her whispers began. The affirmations were cheesy, and they rendered Alicia self-conscious.

"I am beautiful. I am strong. I am vibrant."

Satisfied, Dani left to prepare dinner.

It was only twenty minutes later when she heard the crash. She dropped an entire can of diced tomatoes in the pot in her haste, splashing herself in the juices. She raced down the hallway to Alicia's office, heart racing in time with her steps. She threw open the door.

Alicia lay on the floor, cradling her bloody hand to her chest. Dani noticed a flash of red on the mirror, but her attention was on Alicia. She rushed over to her and inspected the cuts. Her knuckles and back of her hand had been sliced open, as well as her arm. The wounds, though apparently shallow, oozed blood freely. Dani scrambled to get her phone.

"I'm fine," Alicia said.

"You're not fine," Dani said. "The doctor said even small cuts—"

"I said I'm fine."

Alicia's clean hand snatched the phone away.

"I just need to stop the bleeding and clean it," she said.

"What happened?"

"Nothing."

"Nothing?" Dani said. She pointed to the mirror. "That's nothing?"

But when she looked up, the mirror was whole. There was no blood or broken glass. Her arm fell to her side. It had been there. She knew it had.

"See?" Alicia said. "Nothing. Now, how about some lentil stew?"

"You're hungry?" Dani asked.

Alicia's lips curved into a smile. The expression left Dani uneasy. She'd never seen Alicia smile like that.

"Ravenous," Alicia said.

****

"The 12-oz New York Strip, please," Alicia said. "Rare."

Dani grimaced but ordered a salad. It was the first time Alicia had ordered meat in front of Dani since Dani became a vegetarian. As long as Alicia was eating, she wasn't going to complain. Besides, the change in diet in recent weeks seemed to have bettered her health. Her skin had lost its ashen complexion, the spark had returned to her eyes, and she'd even managed to gain a few pounds. The only thing the new diet seemed to have no effect on was her hair, but the treatments would end soon. The progress had shocked the doctors, but Dani had hoped for Alicia's recovery.

"You don't have to just order a salad," Alicia said. "You're basically skin and bones at this point. You could use something heartier."

Dani offered a smile, but she couldn't think of a comeback. When the waitress brought their food, Dani's salad remained untouched as she gazed at Alicia. Her girlfriend lifted her entire steak up in the air with her hands, attracting the attention of several other patrons. She tore off chunks of it with her teeth. The juices flowed down her chin. The juices splattered against the plate and Alicia's pink jacket. At this point, most of the patrons averted their gaze, though a thick and heavy silence hung in the air as all conversation around them ceased.

Dani's smile wavered.

Later that night, Dani woke in the middle of the night to find Alicia had left the bed. She made her way down the hallway, stopping at the office door when she heard a voice. It didn't sound like Alicia. It was deeper, raspy. Then, Alicia's voice.

"I am healthy," Alicia said. "I am strong."

The next few sentences were guttural, foreign. They didn't sound like words, though it was clearly Alicia's voice. Dani opened the door and turned on the light to find Alicia sitting in front of the mirror. There was no one else in the room. Dani shook her head. It was two in the morning, and she had been hearing things.

"What?" Alicia asked.

"Come back to bed," Dani said.

Alicia stood up, fingers brushing the mirror.

"I feel so much better, Dani," she said. "Those affirmations really help, you know?"

Dani's eyes were on the mirror. She thought she saw something in the corner of the room, a shadow, but when she looked for it, there was nothing.

****

Alicia's strength improved almost daily. If anything, she seemed stronger than she'd ever been. She'd given up hiding her carnivorous diet from Dani's prying eyes, and now she ate rare steaks at least once a week. It was revolting to Dani, but she had grown afraid. Alicia's gaze seemed darker, analyzing. Dani would often look up to find Alicia staring at her with narrowed eyes, lips twisted in a snarl. Of course, the moment she'd look, Alicia would laugh it off and pretend that she'd never done anything of the sort. It was all in Dani's head.

Everything was in Dani's head, including the raspy voice and the guttural language she still heard in the office. But Alicia no longer left the door unlocked. She'd spent so much time in the office that Dani typically had only five minutes or so at most each day to look at the mirror. She'd looked for some sort of electronic device at first, maybe a cell phone Alicia didn't want her knowing about despite her insistence that cell phones were annoying. Maybe now that she had recovered, and Dani was still haggard and depressed, she'd found someone else.

Then there was the mirror. Dani had looked into it for hours during a particularly long nap Alicia took the day before, trying to catch a glimpse of whatever Alicia may have been talking to. She'd listened for anything—words, breathing. There had only been silence. She had sometimes wondered if maybe, just maybe, there was something wrong with the mirror. Alicia's sudden recovery had been miraculous, according to the doctors.

But what if it had been something else?

That was silly, though. Dani knew everything was just the result of her sleep deprivation. Couldn't that cause one to hear voices and become exceedingly paranoid?

One evening, she'd chosen to surprise Alicia with a chocolate cake. Alicia had holed herself up in the office again, but perhaps Dani's excellent baking skills would lure her out. She worked on the cake for a good two hours before frosting it.

She'd never bothered to change out of her pajamas, a tank top and pajama bottoms. She hadn't even bothered to bathe. Her teeth were unbrushed, her nails short and ragged from picking up her old habit of nail-biting. There was no point in trying to look pretty anymore. Alicia had basically come back from the dead, but she hadn't really come back to Dani.

She felt hot breath on the nape of her neck.

"What are you doing?" Dani asked.

"Looking at what you're doing," Alicia replied.

Dani recognized the playful tone, the way Alicia's fingers trailed down her exposed arm. She leaned into the touch, having missed the days of peppermint and card games at one in the morning. Alicia kissed her neck, then trailed kisses down to her exposed shoulder.

She nipped the flesh she found there, just like Dani liked. Dani sighed, and then she screamed.

Alicia jumped back, startled.

"What's wrong?" she asked.

"You *bit* me," Dani said.

"Barely."

"You broke the skin!"

"Don't be such a baby," Alicia said. "Are you coming to bed or not?"

"I think I'll work on this cake," Dani said.

Alicia eyed her with annoyance but returned to the office. When she was gone, Dani hurried to disinfect the wound. As she passed the office, she heard the raspy voice again. Her eyes were wide. She'd never heard it during the day.

"Just tell me what I need to do," Alicia said.

The stress overwhelmed Dani. Her gut twisted, and she promptly ran to the bathroom to vomit.

****

"What are you doing?"

Dani ignored Alicia and took another photo of the mirror. When her girlfriend snatched the camera from her, she finally looked up.

"What's it look like?" Dani asked. "We're selling the mirror."

She knelt to grasp a black sheet that rested at her feet. She threw it over the mirror, and for a moment, she had a feeling as though a weight had been lifted. Or a gaze had been covered.

"Get away from there," Alicia said.

Dani rose to her feet to face her. Rage was so foreign in Alicia's features that it took Dani a moment to recognize the emotion. Her voice wavered when she spoke.

"What are you hiding?" she asked.

"I'm deleting those pictures," Alicia said. "We're not selling my mirror."

"I hear you talking to it," Dani said. "Whispering to it. Those words don't sound like affirmations anymore."

"What do they sound like, then?" Alicia asked.

"Like some other language, Alicia. You never even took a foreign language!"

"Mind your own business."

"What is your problem?"

Alicia's fist struck her in the mouth, and she fell over. Her arms instinctively raised to cover her face. Alicia pounced on her, and her other fist pounded into her arms over and over. The sickening sound of her fist meeting Dani's flesh filled the room, and Dani's eyes locked onto the mirror. For a moment, she could swear the figure on top of her reflection didn't resemble Alicia at all, but some sort of dark shadow. Her head ached, and it was likely she had just been hit too hard.

When Alicia rose, Dani scrambled into a sitting position and moved to the other side of the room. Her jaw ached from the blows, and her eyes were wide. She touched her lips, and her fingers came back red. Alicia had never intentionally hurt her. Alicia, the person who cried when one of her fish died. Alicia, the person who held a funeral for their dead cactus.

A small bit of blood lingered on Alicia's fist. She made no move to apologize. When Dani spoke, her own voice cracked in her sudden panic.

"What the hell is your problem?"

Alicia still said nothing.

"You *hit* me," she said. "Get out."

"Where would I go?" Alicia asked.

Dani shook as she gazed at her girlfriend with wonder.

"Do you think I care about that right now?"

"I think you do."

Dani clenched her jaw. She was confused, angry, hurt. She didn't know what to say or do in this situation. She'd never thought it would actually happen to her. Her head was so full of noise and rage that she couldn't handle the argument on top of everything else.

Still, she remembered the woman she'd argued with over a silly card game. She remembered the woman who had broken down in her arms and sobbed after her leukemia diagnosis. She remembered the woman who often attempted to make her breakfast with no culinary skills whatsoever. She remembered the voice that had breathed poetry into her ear.

Then, she remembered the mirror.

She did care, as much as she hated to admit it to herself. She couldn't force Alicia out this late in the evening, not before she'd found a place to stay. Her jaw clenched, teeth grinding along with her sudden burst of self-hatred for her weakness.

"Sleep on the couch, then," Dani said. "I want you gone tomorrow. You and your precious mirror. Understand?"

Alicia said nothing, and Dani stood to brush by her. When she glanced back over her shoulder, she noticed Alicia bringing her fist to her mouth.

"What are you doing?" she asked.

Alicia spun around, and her hand returned to her side. The smear of Dani's blood lingered on her hand. Dani's face twisted in disgust.

"I want you gone tomorrow," she said again.

Alicia gave no indication that she'd heard her. In a huff, Dani returned to her bedroom to read. After all she'd done for Alicia: the schooling she'd put off, the two jobs she'd worked, the mountains of bills she'd paid all by herself, the stupid mirror she'd bought.

Her fingers hovered over the page. The mirror. Tomorrow, she'd break it. She'd shatter it and sweep up the pieces. She was too tired and aching to do it now, but in the morning, she'd be fully rested. She'd destroy it. The thought soothed her into sleep.

She woke to the sensation that something was biting her.

Dani's eyes fluttered open as she shook off the cobwebs of sleep. The pain grew more and more intense as awareness returned to her. Wet, tearing sounds reached her ears. As the pain finally struck her, she screamed.

She tried to pull away, but whatever had her held fast. The pain was in her arm, that much she was sure of. As her eyes adjusted to the darkness, she caught sight of Alicia. She was crouched over Dani, pinning her with her body as she ripped small chunks of flesh from her arm with her teeth. Dani's fist struck her over and over, but she didn't move. Dani reached beside her to grab the bedside lamp, and she slammed it over Alicia's head. Finally, Alicia let go.

Dani had time to get up and move away from the bed. Blood oozed from her arm.

"Dani, I can be well again," Alicia said.

"Get away from me!"

Alicia lunged for Dani and sank her teeth into her other arm. She ripped a small chunk from it, and Dani screamed. She thrashed about in Alicia's embrace, but the other woman was far stronger than she'd ever been. She moaned with each bite of Dani's flesh, and Dani became increasingly aware that whatever was eating her, it wasn't Alicia.

No, Alicia hadn't been *her* Alicia in weeks.

The pain overwhelmed her. It seared through her body, singing her nerves with each bite. The bites were so small, so tentative, as though Alicia was savoring each one.

Dani finally broke free and raced out of the bedroom. She scrambled for a weapon. Anything would do. She settled for a hammer that she'd left behind after hanging up some pictures. She couldn't hear Alicia's steps on the carpet, but her eyes had adjusted well to the dark. So she waited for the monster.

Alicia stumbled into the room as though intoxicated. She turned on a light. Dani's blood stained her face and clothes.

"I can be beautiful again," she said. "You want that, don't you, Dani?"

She rushed at Dani, and Dani brought the hammer down. She brought it down over and over, bathing herself in the sickly blood of the monster that had once been her girlfriend. She slammed the hammer down even after the body beneath her stilled and the skull cracked open. She stood there for a long time after, panting and gazing down at the bloody monster beneath her.

This isn't Alicia's blood, she thought. *This isn't her body.*

She dropped to her knees, vomited, and collapsed onto her side. She stared at the wall, eyes tracing the splatter of blood. After what felt like an eternity, she rose to her feet, hammer in hand. She left to bandage her arms.

****

She wasn't sure what it was—the mirror, that is. But it had something to do with what had happened to Alicia. With the adrenaline from her kill still pumping in her veins, she drew the hammer back.

She smashed it into the mirror. The shards flew out and cut her arms, but the mirror appeared whole no matter how many times she struck it. She caught her reflection: wide, watery eyes with bags under them, thin frame from weeks of little eating, ashen skin.

She pressed her hand to the mirror, smearing her blood to block out the reflection of her face.

The blood disappeared as the mirror drank, and, for the first time in weeks, Dani felt ravenous.

The End

Dream Scape by Marc Shapiro

I hear screams
Under the earth
I see eyes
Piercing
Bloodshot
Looming out of the dark
I see bodies
Lifeless
Bloated
Drained
Floating in agony
Like a horrid, twisted crucifix
In repose
Down a silent stream
I see black on black
In never ending relief
It is all too much
I am tired
It is time to sleep
And to dream

I am No Witch
by
Matthew Wilson

It's a terrible thing to be an old woman at Halloween. The children call me a witch and throw eggs at my window. They write the awful word on my porch and push burning trash through my letterbox. I phone their mothers, but they're disinterested or don't return my calls at all.

Witches are vile things from fantasy stories, and it hurts me as an ex-teacher to be accused of this, especially with the recent murders. I loved children when I was young and wanted to help them. I even tell the devils beheading my roses today to go home before the dark comes, but they don't listen.

My mother said monsters only come out at night.

I wasn't blessed with my own kids, and given the hate this town shines on me, maybe that is best, for the humiliation is terrible. I wouldn't wish old age on anyone. My house is made of brick, not candy, and I cannot help the hideousness of my face.

My neighbors whisper stories of my dear, dead Harry to their children. They laugh and sing about how he went mad, tried to kill me, and burnt my face. I stopped trying to cover it with makeup long ago, but my scars only add fuel to this witch nonsense.

Only evil things burn.

I like to eat in but must order out as supposed *normals* do. The minimum traffic of food deliveries at my door raises the children's certainty that my oven is filled with their cooked brothers and sisters.

I have received no Hansel and Gretel here. Only hate.

Now I hate Halloween. Despite their fear of me, I still phone the children's parents from time to time, seeking unity and to be invited into their homes.

Without their rare good manners, I would starve. My talons would rust and my teeth would fall out.

Only at the end do the few realize what I actually am.

And it is certainly no witch.

The End

Beneath the Moonshine by Baishampayan Seal

moonlight flooding the night
can't tell what it makes
darker
the lurking nocturnal eyes or
the nameless city without life or hope

moon: old lady, grown pale
not from a loveless life, but
from beholding the beasts' fangs
piercing lost travelers' skins in crippling repetitions
Shelley never knew the truth

full moon growing crimson
like the flesh strip
about to drop from my canine

gloomy half moon
incapacitated, I starve
in the body of a half-wolf.

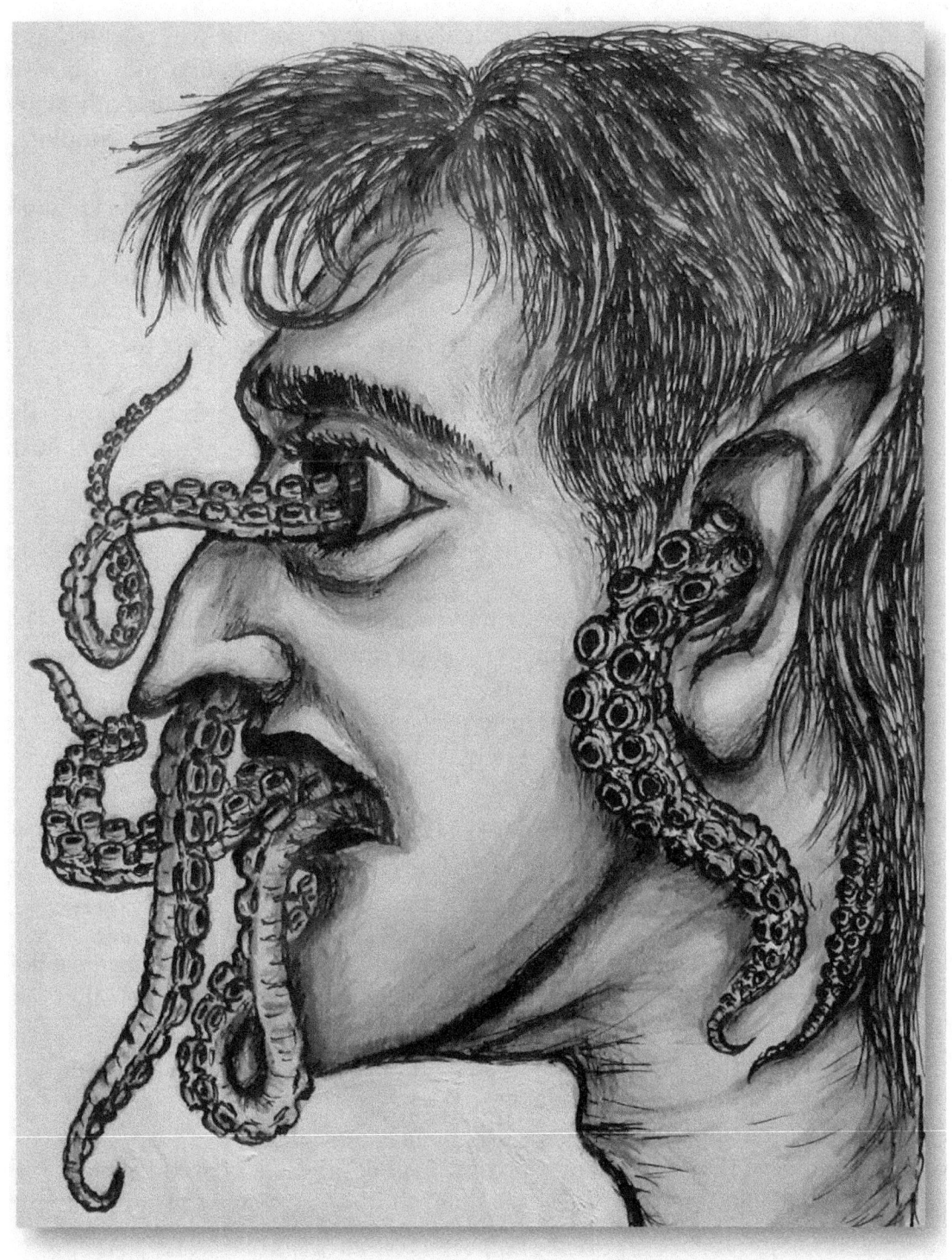

Hearts Rule
by
Rod Marsden

Priestess Helga had just finished her review of the boys she had been tasked to evaluate. Thirteen were on the cusp and could either become knights or mavericks. She was wondering what to do about them when Priestess May approached her. "You have boys on the cusp, too?" she asked.

"Yes." Priestess Helga sighed. "I'll have to think hard about what to do with each of them. I wouldn't want any child to be condemned to fight dragons when they should be running a business somewhere."

"Most of those on the cusp we make into mavericks will eventually become knights anyway," offered Priestess May, "so what we do with them here doesn't really matter."

"I suppose you're right. Suppose these boys are on the cusp and find they can't handle the responsibilities of being even a minor maverick. In that case, they will, sooner rather than later, be downgraded to knight status." Priestess Helga had been involved in enough of these evaluations over the years to know this to be true.

"Some of us priestesses have gotten together to make figuring out what to do with those on the cusp more fun." Priestess May smiled a thin smile. "It's a card game. Aces high. A royal flush of hearts wins every time. Are you in?"

"Gambling for money is against the law." Priestess Helga was firm on this.

"Oh, we don't play for money," said Priestess May. "We play for the lives of the boys on the cusp."

"So the right cards mean a boy gets to be a maverick and has a great life. The wrong cards mean the boy gets to have a shorter life, battling dragons. Is that right?" Priestess Helga was open-mouthed shocked at the implications.

"Five players," said Priestess May, "four to lose a hand and one to win a hand. And so, four boys will become knights and one a maverick. We play until we run out of boys. How many have you got?"

"I have, as the 21st-century people might say, a baker's dozen." Priestess Helga sighed, not caring to say thirteen since that number was once more regarded as unlucky. "I'm not sure I should be doing this."

"You believe in the Great Goddess, don't you?" said Priestess May.

Priestess Helga looked at her white robes and then at Priestess May. "Of course, I do!"

"Then let the Great Goddess decide the fate of these lads through the cards," said Priestess May. "You can't get fairer than that."

Priestess May took Priestess Helga to a backroom in a popular restaurant. There she met three other priestesses sitting around a pinewood table.

"A new recruit," said a pudgy priestess. "My name's Priestess Ruth."

"We needed to have five to get things moving." A tall priestess offered Priestess Helga a seat. "The name's Priestess Holly. We have crisps, peanuts, and beer. If you want something milder, we have soft drink. Shall we get started?"

"How does this work?" asked Priestess Helga, sitting down. Priestess May also took a seat.

"You have the list of boys you don't know what to do with?" Priestess Ruth waved a list she had in front of her. "You tell us the name of the kid you're playing for, and we all do the same. Then it's up to the cards what happens to them. A successful hand means you put a tick beside the boy's name on the sheet you have with the boys' names. If you lose, you put a cross beside the boy's name. A tick and the boy will be a maverick. A cross, and he will be a knight. And no cheating!"

"I'm not sure if I want to do this!" cried Priestess Helga.

"Don't wimp out now," said Priestess May. "I'll deal." She grabbed the cards which were on the centre of the table, shuffled, and dealt.

"Paul," said Priestess Holly. "He's so-so at math, poor swimmer."

"Toff," said Priestess May. "He's lousy at math but good at English and history."

"Grant," said Priestess Ruth. "He's nowhere in English but okay at football."

"Aayan," said a dark-skinned, blue-eyed priestess Helga found out later was called Priestess Fran. "He's good at everything except science."

"Abel," said Priestess Helga. "He's awful at math, but excellent at technical drawing."

Priestess Helga won with three aces, which allowed Able, with a tick, to go on to become a maverick.

"You're a lucky beginner." Priestess Holly smiled and shook her head at Priestess Helga. "It won't last."

Priestess Helga then went on a losing streak. She was not keen on betting with her last boy but was urged to do so.

"You can't stop now. It wouldn't be right." Priestess May's voice was firm.

Priestess Helga took a sip of beer, and Priestess Ruth dealt the cards.

"Frank," said Priestess Holly, "Another loser at math."

"Russel," said Priestess May. "He spent half of last semester at home with a broken leg."

"Henry," said Priestess Ruth. "He failed at metalwork and technical drawing."

"I fold," said Priestess Fran. "I've run out of boys."

"Ernest," said Priestess Helga. "He is good at everything, except biology."

Helga signed deeply, looking at her sheet with all the crosses and only one tick. She then gazed at her cards: five hearts and two aces.

"Here!" she said, presenting them. "Now, I can give Ernest a tick, and he can be a maverick. With further luck, he will never have to be downgraded to knight and face dragons in battle." On her sheet, she now had two ticks out of thirteen. "I'm out!"

Priestess Holly and Priestess Ruth played on; they still had lads to sort out. Priestess Helga finished her beer, ate a handful of crisps, and left. Priestess May followed her out.

"So how was it?" asked Priestess May.

"Fine," replied Priestess Helga. "Do you and the others do this every time?"

"When we get five players, we do." Priestess May smiled her thin smile.

"And you really think the Great Goddess makes the right decisions through the cards?" asked Priestess Helga.

"Of course!" answered Priestess May. "Don't you?"

The End

Every Day I Carry my Mother's Cross and my Father's Worries
by Samuel Junior Irusota

Forgive me for there is a story behind this poem
In my father's house
death was an unwelcomed guest
these days going to church is no longer a sin.
Here dreams do come true
for those who wake up early and pursue them. Tonight
I hold my mother's portrait as a memory of silence
and while I sleep
I light them up as candles in my dreams. Sometimes
night used to be a lonely time for soft hearted boys
my father's ghost never stops singing a mournful song. Everyday
I carry my mother's cross and my father's worries
I rub them together with ashes
and say a silent prayer
they say a leaf does not fall from a tree without God's consent
maybe I defied the laws of heaven
I am that leaf.

God Complex by Marc Shapiro

I am patient zero
I'm the one to praise
I'm the one to blame
Because way back
Before time
And rational thought
Became crude history
On cave walls
I gave up meat for blood
And day for night
I was the one
Who started it all

Haiku I by Denny E. Marshall

small robots inside
need change from virus diet
turn into zombies

The Crocodile Pit
by
Todd Hanks

In the sultry, mosquito-swarming air of the Florida everglades, there was a roadside diner and bar where the old man Kenner fed the people he had murdered to the crocodile pit behind the restaurant. The few tourists they got as customers and the locals liked to watch the reptiles snap and swing their tails, their skin as scaly as the bark on swamp trees.

"Many people deserve to die," Kenner told Melissa. "I'm like an angel of the Lord, serving a termination sentence for sinners. I know you understand, because of what you done. And I ain't judging you in no way. You're an angel, too. Since you showed up to work for me, the diner seems like a little bit of heaven. You've made an old man feel young again, and I didn't think anything could do that ever again. You're my angel, and if I were thirty years younger, I'd ask you to get hitched."

Melissa had often heard the warning bell when she was in the mental asylum. The warning bell from her junior high, before she had dropped out of school. It had rung one minute before the kids were late for class. Now the warning bell would ring in her head, and she knew she had to get out of the mental hospital. She had to get out before it was too late.

The young, pretty woman often sang in her padded room. She would sit and rock on her bed, which was fastened to the cold tile of the floor. Then one day, she got her break. A nurse left the door ajar. The nurse was a person Melissa hated as much as she had hated anything in her life. A smirking nurse, full of insults, often slapped Melissa around when bringing meals to the young woman. She would tease the girl mercilessly, telling her she was lined up for shock treatment. Melissa could feel the nurse's jealousy of her beauty. And Melissa knew she was beautiful. She had been told so many times by men. But this did her no good locked up.

That day, the nurse accidentally left the cell door unlocked. Melissa slipped up behind the asylum worker and wrapped her hands around the woman's throat. "You die, bitch," Melissa said quietly. Soon it was over, and the vicious nurse lay sprawled on the polished tile. Melissa took off the woman's outfit and put it on herself. Then she walked out. It was easy, late night, and she only passed a couple of workers, none of whom knew her. She had also taken the nurse's keys and a surprisingly large amount of bills in the woman's purse. She had heard the nurse before telling the doctor about her new car, a brand-new Mercedes-Benz. Melissa went to the parking lot, climbed into the Mercedes, and drove from Alabama deep into the Florida everglades. She met Kenner, got a free backroom in the diner to stay in, and worked as a waitress. Sometimes after Kenner would kill one of the locals, she would help him feed the body parts to the crocodiles in the pit. She felt she owed the old man that.

Bobby Joe was a regular in Kenner's diner. Every night, he would get plastered. His drink was Irish whiskey. He and Melissa were alone in the bar the night he raped her. He forced her to the floor in the back of the wooden bar, after punching her several times. The next day, he was surprised to get a phone call from her at work.

"Hi, Bobby Joe. How are ya doing? I've been missing you."

"I'm surprised to hear from you, Melissa," he said in a confused manner.

"Truth is, Bobby Joe, I secretly liked what you did to me last night. I've had fantasies, but never experienced such a thing. Could we get together tonight?"

And they did. This time they went into the spare room Melissa stayed in. After undressing, they crawled into her single bed. "You can hit me again if you want," the young woman whispered.

And Bobby Joe raised a fist above her face. At the same time, Melissa slipped an open pocket knife from under her pillow. She had found the knife in Kenner's room. Bobby Joe's penis came off like cutting through butter. As he screamed, she made one more slice, this time across the throat. Kenner ran into the room when he heard the racket.

"Oh, Melissa! Well, you did him up right. Never did like the man. Anytime him and another drunk wanted to fight, they decided to meet in my diner. Hurry, we gotta get the body out to the croc pit. Help me carry him."

The crocodiles never left evidence of a murdered person. Maybe a few shreds of clothing or some jewelry to clean up. That was it. Kenner liked to say that the crocodiles were more than efficient.

The next day a local policeman showed up. Melissa was worried he knew something about Bobby Joe's disappearance. However, she was surprised when the cop was friendly to her.

"Honey, I got curious about the car you drive. It seemed awful new and expensive for a cocktail waitress in this dive. I ran a check and found out it was stolen, and I found out from where. I have to take you back to the hospital now, Melissa. A lot of people there will be glad to see you. They've missed you, girl."

The phone rang from the back of the bar, and Kenner answered. "It's for you, Officer Davis," he hollered. "Someone from the station."

"You come on back with me now, honey," said the policeman.

As she walked back to the phone, accompanying Officer Davis, Kenner slipped a pocket knife into her hand and nodded at her. Kenner walked with them. "Yes, I got her here now," the policeman said into the phone. "I'll be bringing her in."

When Melissa slit the man's throat, the cut was not deep enough to kill immediately. The cop stumbled back against the pay telephone, drawing his pistol. A shot went off like a sonic boom, but the bullet did not hit Melissa. Instead, Kenner dropped dead on the floor, a hole of crimson in his forehead. Then the policeman fell to the warped wood floor and joined Kenner in death.

Melissa could hear the warning bell pounding its chime like a death toll in her head. She couldn't take any more and knew she had to get out for good. They would come looking for her, she knew, and she was sure they would catch her. It was all over.

Melissa took a paper from the bar and wrote a suicide note. She walked out to the crocodile pit and took off all her clothes, throwing them into the pit. Then she hung her shoes on nails on the wooden fence and stuck the note on a nail. For a long while, she just stood and stared at the reptiles' teeth, imagining them tearing into her flesh. Then she took off, and it was all over.

The two policemen stood at the crocodile pit, shaking their heads. "I wonder why Kenner killed a police officer. My theory is that he was in love with this young woman. And he couldn't bear to see her took away from him. I saw her a few times in the bar," he said. "She was one damn good-looking woman."

"Yep," said the other officer. "She seemed sweet, too, even though she was crazy as a loon, I understand. Most people like her commit suicide. And she, of course, didn't want to go back to the asylum. Who would? She probably didn't see any reason to live. I guess there's no good way to die, but by my God, she chose a horrible one. Torn to pieces by crocs. This whole thing is a crying shame."

Melissa chugged down the highway in Kenner's old red pick-up truck, leaving the Florida everglades for good. The truck had been a spare, stored for years in a shed out back. She knew the police wouldn't notice it missing. The sunlight bounced off the dirty truck hood, and she was thinking of what a pleasant day it was. The air felt warm as a blanket around her. *I'm going to miss Kenner*, she thought. Melissa remembered slipping the bloody knife into his dead fingers. *I fooled them again*, she thought. *I know I did. I always do.*

The End

Sonnet of Arachne by Todd Hanks

Of mortals weaving looms of tapestries,
Arachne by far wove the fairest art.
The nymphs would leave the deepest forest parts
and fountains just to view the rare beauties.

The maiden insulted a deity,
Minerva, goddess of embroidery,
and said that she could weave a finer scene,
upon the cloth connected to her beam.

Arachne then received an awful fate,
forever to be in a spider's guise.
She watched the world from eight remorseful eyes,
her regretful feelings felt too late.

From then her pictures would adorn a web,
and she would dangle from a silken thread.

Haiku II by Denny E. Marshall

plane explodes in sky
shock as you look up and see
falling knife shipment

Ivan & Goddess of Time
by
Marge Simon

After dinner, Ivan is out for a smoke, as he's wont to do if weather permits. The oaks are limed in shadows, the heavens ablaze with points of light. This night seems different, full of portent. He strikes a match to his pipe, wondering if he might discover some new constellation of his own invention. But the flame goes out as a woman materializes, the sexiest young woman he's ever seen. She appears to float his way, holding an object lit with an otherworldly glow. Ivan stares with pipe unlit, wondering where she comes from, and why here, to his back yard.

"I come to share," she says, revealing a golden hour glass, its top half almost empty. Trembling, Ivan touches it. "I know who you are, gorgeous. You're an angel, come to tell me that my time here is at an end." His eyes narrow. "Is this not so?"

"Wrong, Ivan! I'm no angel, I'm the Goddess of Time. As to why I'm here—oh!"

Ivan instantly snatches the glass out of her hand, turning it back over as he does. "Say no more, you beautiful broad. I get to live as long as I want, now. With another lifetime ahead, I can prepare myself to be president of our nation. I can have all the sexy women I wish, starting with you."

The goddess begins laughing. "Do you actually believe I'd bring you my sacred Glass of Hours? I have a bet with the God of Fools that you'd do something like this. He thought you'd beg me for a kiss, maybe ask me to sleep with you. Hah!"

"I was just about to propose both of those things," says Ivan. "But you are saying this is a fake?"

"It surely is, but you're smarter than I'd thought, Ivan. Anyway, it doesn't matter now."

Ivan stares speechless as the lovely goddess unhinges her jaw. "It gets boring, being a Goddess. Sometimes I need a change of pace. I'm moonlighting as a vampire this evening; that's what I wanted to share, little man."

The End

Bane of Full Moons by Matthew Wilson

No man is afraid with a bloody blade
Trusting your life to a knife.
Defending yourself in a moonlit glade
Against the transformation of your wife.

When Shadows Scream
by
Lee Clark Zumpe

MACON – An Oak Ridge woman was critically injured in an early morning accident on County Road 411.

According to the Bibb County Sheriff's Office, the woman – whose name has not been released pending notification of family – was southbound on a two-lane section of the road when she encountered a large mound of loose gravel. Authorities believe the debris field may have been created hours earlier when state work vehicles traveled through the area en route to a construction site on I-75.

The woman apparently swerved to avoid a collision and lost control of her vehicle. The vehicle, found more than 50 feet off the pavement along a creek bed, impacted with a tree.

The victim was taken to Northside Hospital for evaluation. A spokesman for the sheriff's office indicated she suffered "catastrophic head injuries" and was not expected to regain consciousness.

****

Byron sat at Savannah's bedside with his chair positioned so that he could rest his hand upon hers. The nurse occasionally stepped into the private room, checked to see if he was comfortable, to see if she needed anything. He spoke for her since she could not answer.

When friends asked about her, he told them she remained "stable." He preferred not to refer to her as "comatose" and winced when attending physicians labeled her condition as a "persistent vegetative state" and expressed doubts over her prognosis. The sneering, unsympathetic doctors at the university hospital had belittled him for not allowing them to let her die on the operating table.

Things had gotten less stressful since Byron moved her to the assisted living center located in the quiet mountain town of Tahlequah, North Carolina.

Byron could disregard the tube that sank beneath her pasty flesh, ignore the monitor on the wall that displayed her vitals. He could forget the bleakness of the sterile room that could not be softened by the most vibrant bouquets or an army of stuffed animals. In six months of extended visits, he had learned to focus his gaze so efficiently that he could deceive himself, briefly, into believing that nothing had happened.

In those fleeting moments, Savannah became his sleeping beauty, his princess, and the world filled with hope.

Her external wounds had long-since healed. Though still fresh in his memory, the bruises she had suffered, the gash across her forehead, the swollen lips caked with blood from the accident had all faded. Her bones had mended. Her internal injuries had been repaired.

Still, life lingered on the periphery. She died sometime after they pulled her from the jagged tangle of metal, plastic and glass that had been her car. Somewhere between the burning wreckage and the emergency room, in a speeding ambulance rushing her to the hospital, her heart stopped. No one could be blamed – they resuscitated her as quickly as possible. A few seconds too late, perhaps. She had been gone a few instants too long and had gotten lost trying to return.

Byron spent every moment he could spare waiting by her side, diligently searching for a sign:

the hint of a smile, the flutter of an eyelid, the twitch of a finger. He whispered secrets to her that only she could know, reminded her of stories they had lived together. He promised not to give up hope.

****

Dr. Donovan Durward arrived at the Alameda Assisted Living Facility shortly after 9:00 p.m. as he did most every night.

"Evening, doctor." Sprightly desk clerk Brina Sellers turned her attention from the Stephen King hardback on the countertop, folding the top corner down before closing the book to mark her place. A student taking morning classes at William Whitley College, Brina had answered a classified ad three months earlier to fill the position. The owner had been charmed by her incurable lightheartedness – the ideal trait to brighten an otherwise cheerless atmosphere. "How's it going?"

"Fine, Brina, fine," Durward said. "Finished this month's invoices yet?"

"Yes sir, all caught up," she said, delighted with her accomplishment. She patted the mountain of file folders neatly stacked between the telephone and computer monitor. "Bad news, though. Nurse Melanie called in sick. She was supposed to be on duty until morning." Brina pouted, cocked her head and raised her eyebrows. "And Elsie can't stay tonight. Doesn't have anyone to watch her kids."

"So I'm on my own?"

"I'll stick around if you'd like." Though genuine, the offer lacked commitment. Durward knew Brina would work overtime when asked, but she had other things to do. "I can cut tomorrow morning's classes if I have to."

"No, that's all right. I can handle things here until Benton comes in."

"If you're sure." She smiled, gathering her belongings. "You've got my number if you need anything. Oh, and don't forget about the new arrival. Elsie can fill you in."

Brina slipped out the front door and into the darkness. Alameda's remote location in the sparsely populated, dense forests west of Tahlequah made it seem more like a hidden artists' retreat than a healthcare center. Its isolation had initially concerned Byron, but the owners had assured him that police and ambulances could reach the location quickly in an emergency, and the calming effect of the natural setting had a therapeutic value for patients, staff members and visiting relatives.

Still, sometimes the detachment from Tahlequah and the associated sense of stifling solitude made the place seem somehow disheartening and almost sinister. The Alameda's unsavory history as a turn-of-the-century insane asylum did little to dispel its endemic melancholy.

Durward, the resident physician at Alameda, stopped by the nurse's station before making his rounds. He assured Elsie that he could manage the facility single-handedly – he had done it several times in the past, for one reason or another. The next nurse would be arriving around 3 a.m.

The doctor regularly visited each patient in the evening, stayed on until midnight or later depending on scheduling demands. Alameda was a small, privately-owned establishment that provided exceptional service with a small, well-trained staff that understood the importance of maintaining a healthy relationship with both the patients and their loved ones.

Byron liked Durward because he spoke to Savannah, treated her like she was conscious and fully aware of her surroundings.

"If you treat them like they aren't here with us, then they have no reason to try to respond," he once told Byron. "Involve them, interact with them, tell them about your day. Try to provoke a response, and some day you might succeed."

Alameda housed a limited number of patients. The refurbished facility had a total of thirteen private apartments – far fewer than the massive Victorian-style complex that once dominated the landscape. Savannah occupied Room 5. The new arrival had taken the only empty room, Room 11. Room 11 had been vacated recently when Mrs. Braunstein, a former professor at William Whitely

College, had passed away unexpectedly. She had been a dweller in Alameda for more than a year following a series of seizures.

The main part of the original facility had burned to the ground back in the late 1920s. Officially, three dozen patients perished, but records had been lost in the blaze, and administrators obstructed all inquiries. During the renovation and restoration that commenced more than three decades later, the remains of more than a hundred victims surfaced during excavation.

Durward reviewed the new patient's file with professional attentiveness. A transfer from Tusgagunee University Hospital in north Georgia, Darnell Jordan had been in a coma for three months following a shooting during a botched robbery. He was unmarried and childless. His mother had made arrangements for his relocation to Alameda but had not personally visited the facility. She left contact information. She faxed the admission forms from Atlanta, leaving the section labeled Anticipated Visitation Schedule completely blank.

Ms. Jordan had sent Darnell to Alameda to die.

Durward did not fault her, did not think less of her for what some might consider callous neglect. Some people remained loyal to their loved ones. Some people could not bear to see them lying dormant as days, weeks, years passed. Visiting reminded them of their powerlessness and their own mortality.

Durward understood. Besides, the lack of attention made things easier on him.

****

Byron awoke shortly after midnight.

He had drifted off sometime after 9:00 p.m. Usually, a nurse would come by and wake him, remind him about visiting hours. Alameda asked families to leave no later than 10.

He rubbed his eyes and glanced at Savannah, still resting quietly, still a portrait of grace and tranquility.

He stuck his head out the door, glared up and down the darkened corridor. Silence and shadow held dominion over the facility. From where he stood, he could see the nurse's station. Elsie had gone home. It appeared that no one had arrived to replace her. Dr. Durward must be poking around the rooms, checking on patients.

Byron wondered why he had not stopped to check on Savannah.

Still groggy, he considered sitting back down in the comfortable chair, propping his legs up on the bedside and dozing off again. He dreaded the drive home along the twisting mountain road, down the mountainside, through the dense forest beneath the unforgiving twilight. Though the temptation to spend the rest of the night with Savannah appealed to him, he decided not to take advantage of the situation. Alameda had rules – best not to endanger Savannah's placement by offending the owners.

Byron kissed his wife on the forehead, wished her sweet dreams and collected his coat.

Before leaving, he wanted to check with the doctor. He liked to get daily updates on her condition, monitor her prescriptions, learn about any new therapies that might hasten her recovery. Basically, their conversations consisted of small talk. Durward reassured him, and he repeatedly professed his dedication to her recuperation. The dialogues may have had no curative impact on Savannah, but they helped Byron sustain his commitment.

He took great care walking down the hallway, trying not to make any noise, trying not to wake any of the patients. Halfway to the nurse's station, he stopped, laughed at himself. Waking a patient here would only win him gratitude, he thought.

Durward stumbled out of a room at the far end of the opposite wing. Tall and bony, with unusually long arms and legs, he closed the door to Room 13. Tucked beneath one arm he carried a box. In the other hand, he held a black canvas bag.

34

Byron thought he saw the bag shudder once, its surface rippling with motion as if something inside squirmed and wriggled as it wrestled for freedom. All kinds of thoughts crept into Byron's head – visions of appalling rodent infestations, images of rats, mice, squirrels and other less palatable furry lurkers.

"Dr. Durward?" Byron lingered in front of the reception desk, his eyes straining to catch another glimpse of the captured mystery. "Is everything all right, Dr. Durward?"

Durward, startled by the sight of a visitor, nearly dropped the bag. The wooden case he had been carrying did fall to the tiled floor, splintering its exterior and spilling its contents. The clatter and clang of metal crashing echoed through the facility like a full tray of silverware being dumped. Byron cringed. The doctor muttered some unintelligible exclamation, something analogous to blue-collar profanities only less plebeian. He tossed the canvas bag into a nearby depository for dirty linens after checking to make sure it was properly sealed.

"That you, Byron?" Durward recovered some of his composure, forced a tentative smile and waved. "You're here late."

"Sorry, sir. I fell asleep. No one woke me."

"Oh, yes, I'm here by myself. The night nurse apparently has a stomach virus." Durward knelt, examined the box. The instruments it had housed lay scattered across the tile.

"Let me help you with that," Byron said, walking down the corridor toward Room 13.

"No, that's all right," Durward said. Byron had already arrived. Byron joined Durward in scanning the hodgepodge of unrecognizable instruments strewn over the floor. The doctor seemed to be taking inventory, searching for specific pieces. "There you are," he said, reaching for what appeared to be an elongated pair of scissors curved at the end. He plucked it from the floor and stashed it in the pocket of his white coat. "Don't want to lose that one."

"I'm so sorry." Byron began to collect other tools randomly, piling them in the damaged container. As he helped gather them, he realized the instruments were not common – they were old, antique. "I'm so sorry, I'll repay you."

"Don't worry, no harm done," Durward said. "It's an old set, but I have several others. The box can be replaced."

"How old is it?"

"It dates back to about 1830, 1840." Durward flipped the top of the box over and showed the manufacturer's engraving. "I collect old surgical sets." The large rosewood case lined with black velvet had corners which were reinforced with brass fittings. It contained a removable tray and instruments for trepanning, eye surgery, amputation and urology. Individual tools included a primitive trephine for drilling into the skull, a trocar for drainage of the body cavity, tourniquets, arterial tweezers, bone files and saws and bone-cutting forceps. "Most of these tools are obsolete," Durward said, noticing Byron's curiosity. "A few, though, haven't changed much in design over the last few hundred years, and could still be used effectively today."

"They look like, like," Byron began, hesitating. He did not want to offend the doctor.

"Like instruments of torture?" Durward read his mind. "It's all right – some of them probably evolved from utensils used in torture chambers." The doctor placed a firm hand on Byron's shoulder, began guiding him down the corridor toward the lobby. "You had better get on the road. I won't say anything to the owners about your being here after visiting hours."

"I'd appreciate it," Byron said. "Good night, Dr. Durward."

"Good night, Byron. Sleep tight."

Walking beneath the unresponsive theater of twilight, its myriad shimmering candles too dim and distant to reveal the faces of far-flung audience members, Byron crossed the nearly vacant parking lot, imagining the day when Savannah would accompany him home. He had played out the scenario many times, hearing her laughter, clasping her warm hand, seeing her smile. His confidence in her recovery remained steadfast most of the time.

Occasionally, he faltered.

He leaned against the side of his car staring at the immeasurable night sky, wondering if Savannah now dwelled in another corner of the vast cosmos, wondering if she missed him and struggled to return. She might never find her way back to him from that black abyss. As often as he had envisioned the moment her eyes would open and her lips would speak his name, recently he had pictured a different future – a sad and lonely life usurped by obsessive devotion and caretaking as he grew older and older, silently waiting for a reunion that would never come to pass.

Byron shook the thought from his mind as he shuffled through his pockets looking for his car keys – keys he had left on the little table in Savannah's room.

****

Durward skulked in the lobby until Byron had disappeared into the parking lot.

Satisfied, he darted back down the corridor and retrieved his harvest from the dirty linen cart. As he plucked the bag from the mound of soiled sheets and sweat-soaked gowns, its contents resumed a fierce struggle, thrashing and clawing at the canvas.

With newly found energy, it vented its plea for freedom in a shrill, bone-chilling screech that echoed throughout the facility.

"Scream all you want. No one here is listening." Durward slung the wriggling sack over his shoulder.

He started toward the door that led to the tunnels beneath Alameda – toward the old depository he had discovered years ago. He paused outside Room 11. Darnell Jordan waited for him. Durward wondered if he dared perform a second excision in one night. Rarely did he have such an opportunity. Rarely did he have the benefit of complete privacy. It had taken him weeks to collect from the gentleman in Room 13.

Glancing at his wristwatch, he decided to chance it. His Masters would reward him generously. His contributions would accelerate their venture, hasten their arrival.

As the door to Room 11 closed behind Durward, Byron punched in the code on the keypad at the lobby door, waited for the buzzer to sound and crept back in to the building to retrieve his keys. Silence and darkness worked in unison to make the interior atmosphere as unsettling as it had ever seemed.

Byron slipped beyond the unattended reception desk, clambered by the nurse's station. He shambled down the corridor and could not help but peer through doors left ajar, study the faces of those shackled to feeding tubes and dependent on ventilators. Pharmaceuticals and machines maintained their bodies while medical science failed to revive their minds. Some elderly patients clung to life tenuously, lingering indefinitely. Younger victims demanded even more sympathy, their lives reduced to endless slumber, perhaps without even the indulgence of dreams.

Byron's keys jingled as his fingers swept them off the windowsill in Savannah's room. For a moment, he forced himself to look upon her as he saw the others – not with a spark of life buried just beneath the surface, but lifeless and distant, detached and inaccessible. He knew that every day she slipped farther away from him. He knew that every day his expectations shrank.

Sometimes, hope was as much a curse as a blessing.

Byron could not resist placing one last goodnight kiss on her warm cheek. He repeated his nightly vow to wait for her recovery, a mantra that had grown tiresome and stale. Tomorrow night, though, he would whisper the same promise.

On the opposite end of the facility, Durward redirected an examination lamp in Room 11 so that it bathed Darnell Jordan in sallow radiance. Darnell's well-defined shadow spilled across the floor, equally as motionless as its source. The doctor, giddy with zeal, pulled back the sheets and scrutinized the comatose body, tracing the flesh, searching for something. He poked and prodded limbs and torso, watched the floor and gauged the reaction of the patient's silhouette.

"There you are," Durward said as he pinched a particular patch of skin on Darnell's shoulder. He fidgeted with it for a moment, fingers fiddling as he tried to pinion the pliant tissue and seize the less tangible, fibrous ethereal strand that connected shadow to host. "I've got you now," he said, grabbing the archaic scissors from his pocket. As the twin blades of that instrument bit into the dark, airy substance and the shadow began to separate, a deafening howl echoed through Alameda. "No point in struggling. You belong to me."

Byron, reaching for the front door, froze. The hideous scream reverberated in the marrow of his bones. Unlike any cry he had ever heard, the harrowing call resonated with fear and desperation and misery.

The razor-sharp cutting edge continued its long, fastidious passage, drifting along an almost unseen seam, detaching the spectral filaments composing the patient's shadow. While Darnell remained static and voiceless, his vaporous doppelganger writhed in agony and terror. Durward gathered the insubstantial material with his free hand, clumping it together with grappling fingers until it became a misty knot of quivering matter. When the archaic scissors completed the excision, Durward returned them to the safety of his pocket.

Standing beside the bed, the doctor turned his attention to the harvested shadow. Holding it in one hand, he relaxed his grip, allowing it to unfurl, to reconstruct itself in its former configuration. Its screams had deteriorated into sporadic whimpers and yelps but it continued to struggle, extending its gummy elongated limbs towards its estranged host.

Byron now stood just outside the door, watching. He clamped a trembling hand across his lips to muffle a gasp of disbelief. Durward manhandled the thing, jerking it away from the comatose patient resting on the bed. Byron's mind strained to make some sense of the scene as his eyes strived to discern a definitive outline of the thing dangling from Durward's grasp. It possessed a tenuous form with no traceable contour and a grayish, semi-transparent composition.

Durward toyed with his new pet like a child torturing a captured animal. With his free hand he fingered the captive, tugging at the stringy shadow fabric and stretching it like pulled taffy. Each moment the thing remained displaced, its cries grew weaker. With every passing minute, its attempts to reunite became less confident and unrelenting as its resolve seemed eclipsed by hopelessness and the acknowledgment of tragedy.

"That's it," Durward said. "Settle down, now. No use in fighting it. You are dead in this world, but you can serve in another."

****

Byron shadowed Durward down a narrow passageway leading to secreted chambers beneath Alameda – a subterranean lair that dated back to the facility's earliest days. Painstakingly excavated, the meandering tunnel reveled in its own overwhelming darkness. Though Durward navigated the oblique path clutching a flickering flashlight, the surrounding gloom absorbed its negligible radiance. Its dull glow scarcely repelled the crypt-like blackness of the place and Byron found it increasingly difficult to focus on the distant shimmer as he struggled to maintain his pursuit.

Just as the pitch threatened to press him into submission, penetrating his pores and saturating his lungs and eclipsing his sanity, Byron recognized a mounting crimson ruddiness infecting the darkness – a pulsing luminosity that only served to make the cavern more miserable.

"Get in there," Durward commanded, emptying the first of two sacks into a deep pit in the floor of the cave. Deep red flames shot forth from the crater and a symphony of screams erupted – tormented shrieks so appalling that Byron winced and turned away. "Quiet, all of you!"

The cries only multiplied and intensified. A dozen separate voices vented unintelligible howls. Each tortured detainee had been stripped of the luxury of language and reduced to grunting and screeching and wailing. Each wretched, pitiable scream conjured images of shackled souls, illegitimately damned and cunningly subjugated, and cast into some abysmal nightmare more deplorable than any traditional conception of hell.

"More slaves to serve your goals," Durward said, preparing to dump Darnell's shadow into the unearthly flames. "Let no one hinder your undertaking. Let no one challenge your dominion. Let no one delay your return." The shadow spilled over the rim of the pit as he tipped the bag, and it clawed at the stony ground. It put up a noble fight before tumbling back into the raging fires. Durward peered over the edge, his scarlet face aglow from the violent inferno.

Byron finally emerged from the darkness, condemning the doctor. Surprised, Durward edged away from the pit. His hands fumbled in his pockets.

"What have you done?"

"Byron – you shouldn't have followed me."

"What have you done with her? Is she down there?" Byron's shifted his gaze toward the gaping hole in the floor of the cave. Drawing closer, he could see a ring of unfamiliar symbols carved into the rock around the opening – strange, alien characters that held no meaning for him. "Where is –"

"No!" Durward shouted, bolting forward. As he lunged, Byron saw the glint of metal in his hand and reacted. "Don't say it! You mustn't say her name!"

Durward's arm swept in a downward, stabbing arc. Byron sidestepped the attack, grabbing the doctor's forearm from below with one hand. With his free hand, he delivered a blow that snapped Durward's arm at the elbow. The antique surgical scissors tumbled to the ground.

"Why?" Byron watched as the doctor, whimpering, collapsed onto the floor of the cavern. "Why can't I say her name?"

"You mustn't," he repeated, writhing in agony. "Their will must be served – arrangements have been made, covenants enacted, promises made." Byron knelt beside the doctor. Though pain twisted his face, his eyes betrayed only regret. "I've failed them," he mumbled, tears streaming. "I'm a disgrace to the bloodline."

"How many have you brought here?" Byron tried to stare into the heart of the fire hidden deep within the pit. "How many patients have you victimized?"

"Don't you see, Byron? They were dead to the world. Here, they serve a purpose. They are builders of a cosmic bridge, disciples of tomorrow's gods."

"They're slaves." Byron grabbed Durward's collar and dragged him toward the pit. "And you're going to join them now. You're going to suffer alongside of all your patients – alongside Savannah."

"No!" Durward flinched and kicked. The flames suddenly burgeoned and Byron backed away from the pit. Durward, too, tried to move away, but unseen forces had already laid claim to him. He screamed as his displeased Masters took possession of him, pulling him into the pit and into damnation.

Even as Durward slipped from view, a single shadow materialized hovering above the flames. It lingered beside Byron for just a moment – long enough to reassure him. He smiled as he felt Savannah's lips brush his forehead.

He found her in her room a short time later. She had no recollection of her enslavement, no memory of anything since the day of the accident.

"I've missed you," Byron said, holding her. Her warmth gave him the strength to do what had to be done. "I have to finish something, sweetheart. I'll be back before dawn. Promise me you'll be here when I get back."

"I promise," she said.

On his way back to the tunnel, Byron stopped at the unattended nurse's station. He slipped behind the desk, shuffled through paperwork. He found what he needed on a clipboard on the wall.

"What are you doing?" Benton, the early morning nurse, stood with his arms folded staring at Byron. "You shouldn't be here – and you shouldn't be behind the desk."

"I'm sorry, Benton – I'll explain everything in a little while," Byron could not conceal his happiness. His smile stretched from ear to ear. "Right now, I'd appreciate it if you could check in on Savannah. I think you'll find her much more talkative than usual."

"She's awake?"

"Yeah, yeah, she's back." Byron headed toward the doorway that led to the tunnels. He carried a list of patient's names in his hand. "Oh, and, Benton – things are probably going to get busy this morning. You might want to call for some help."

****

TAHLEQUAH – Authorities are baffled by the simultaneous recovery of more than a dozen comatose patients at the privately operated Alameda healthcare center. Staff members are referring to the event as nothing short of miraculous.

Family members began arriving at the center yesterday to be reunited with their loved ones. Some patients had been unconscious for several years and were not expected to recover.

In an unrelated and developing story, one of the center's resident physicians, Donovan Durward, has been reported missing. Alameda's owners could not be reached for comment on either matter.

The End

Ales Stenar by Lee Clark Zumpe

faceless ancestors toil in
bronze age fields across Europe
erecting megalithic monuments

imprinting cryptic messages
that echo across millennia
and beguile distant descendants.

near Kaseberga they still stand
provoking dubious speculation
about gods in fiery chariots

providing technological innovations
in return for veneration
and the promise of immortality.

Support Group
by
Margaret L. Carter

"I believe all but one of our scheduled participants are present." Dr. Roger Darvell, the psychiatrist conducting the group therapy session, checked his watch and continued, "Please, if you will, each of you begin by telling us why you're here." He nodded to the young-looking man in jeans and a black leather jacket on his right.

"The same reason as most of you, I suppose." The speaker ran a hair through his curly hair, chestnut with golden highlights. "To find a cure for this diabolical—compulsion."

A fair-skinned lady with luxuriant ebony hair, the only woman present, said with a brittle laugh, "Sir Nicholas, you talk like a priest! Nature knows nothing of good or evil. I'm here because my lovers cannot seem to understand this truth." Her haunting, dark eyes brimmed with tears as she went on in her faintly Germanic accent, "Always they reject me when they discover my—condition. Love is so painful—my self-esteem suffers so dreadfully—"

The man on her right, equally pale and dark-haired, dressed like a seventeenth-century cavalier, said only, "Attempted suicide. Jumped into a volcano."

The others winced.

"I, also, by walking into sunlight," said the somber black man next to him, tall and imposing in his flowing, black cloak. "And why they will never let us rest, those monsters of greed in your golden western land—" He glared around the circle.

A man in an Inverness caped coat, leaning on a wolf's-head cane, raised his deep-set, shadowed eyes to survey his fellow patients. "I, too, seek a cure. I've almost had it several times, but it always proved to be an illusion."

"Fools!" burst out a tall, old man with a flowing mustache and a strongly aquiline profile. "You, trying to throw away your gift of immortality. And you, begging to be 'cured' of your powers. I am elder and greater than most of you, so perhaps your folly shouldn't surprise me. But you, Sir Nicholas—not only scorning your gifts, but prostituting them to enforce the petty laws of these ephemeral creatures. Why haven't you learned better in your eight centuries?"

"Just Nick," said the young-looking man. "Maybe I've learned more than you have."

"If you feel that way, Count," Dr. Darvell asked, "why are *you* here?"

The elder's lip curled in a disdainful snarl. "Your modern medical charlatans would call it an identity crisis or perhaps multiple personality disorder. Those mountebanks beyond the sunset trouble my peace, also. They have made me a warlord, a bloodthirsty beast, a defender of the faith, a cruel tyrant, a melancholy aristocrat, a romantic lover, or sometimes the butt of their crude jests on boxes of breakfast food for children. Some even take me for a sentimental idiot like you, Black Prince. But whatever I am, I chose my fate and embrace it without regret."

The black man rose from his chair, fists clenched and fangs bared. "That gives you no right to force your condition on others, as you did to me."

The other replied with a ghastly grin, "Why, I did you a favor. Have you not come to appreciate it yet?" He directed a seated bow to the woman. "Countess Karnstein, at least, understands our inherent superiority, even if she does have a regrettable tendency to whine."

The Countess bared her teeth in a feral hiss.

Dr. Darvell raised a warning hand. "Please, Count, exercise simple courtesy. We're here to listen to each other non-judgmentally, not fight among ourselves. I believe one thing we can all agree on is the need for solidarity in the face of the derogatory stereotypes and racist harassment suffered by our kind. Let's hear from someone else, please."

The cavalier spoke up. "The Prince is absolutely right. This existence is a burden. When my curse condemned an innocent girl to a terrible death, I knew honor demanded I end my unnatural life. But they won't allow us to rest."

"Well, Sir Francis," the Count said, "if an active volcano wasn't enough to terminate your 'curse,' maybe you should learn to enjoy it."

"Enjoy being chased from town to town by stake-wielding fanatics?"

"At least you," said the man with the cane, "have been spared waking after two centuries sealed in a coffin to a world you cannot comprehend."

The black man nodded. "How true, Mr. Collins. I shall never forget the horror of my first encounter with Los Angeles traffic. Or the shock of that insidious invention, the camera. How was I to know it would betray me as surely as a mirror?"

"Consider yourself fortunate you weren't unearthed as I was," said Collins, "by a treasure-hunting halfwit I had to depend on for my knowledge of the modern era. And it hasn't helped that I can't overcome my tendency to see every woman who attracts me as a reincarnation of my long-lost love."

The black Prince said, "I've had that problem, too."

Dr. Darvell interjected, "That's not an uncommon fixation. Relationships can often be problematic for us. Would anyone else care to share on this topic?"

With a voluptuous pout, the Countess tossed her head. "So many times I have loved, and always tragically, thanks to those hypocritical filmmakers you mentioned." She glanced at the Count. "They enrich themselves at my expense, while condemning me to stake and fire for my 'wanton' behavior."

"Granted," said the psychiatrist, "the collective unconscious and popular culture harbor mixed messages regarding our lifestyle."

"Even gay and lesbian support organizations reject me," the Countess sighed. "They insist I must be exploiting my lovers."

The doctor looked around the circle. "Anyone else? I believe you've experienced problems in this area, Nick."

"I won't consider becoming involved with a woman until I'm cured." He shook his head despairingly. "I've even tried a twelve-step program. No luck."

"Do you consider living on refrigerated cattle blood such a terrible handicap, or curse, as to disqualify you for intimate relationships?"

"Since Natalie thinks that diet is a roadblock to a cure, and she's the woman I—well—"

Collins frowned at the young-looking man. "You're wasting your time. I've also had a—relationship—with a female scientist attempting to cure me. The results have been disastrous."

"Sir Nicholas—Nick," the Count said with an ironic smile, "your friend might not see your condition as a curse if you introduced her to certain benefits associated with it."

Nick bared his fangs, eyes glowing.

The doctor again held up his hand to silence them. "Calm yourself. We can't evade what we all know from experience, the erotic dimension of feeding."

"If you're suggesting Nat would ever want that kind of perverted thrill—"

A red glint sparked in the Count's eyes. "Are you implying that all the young ladies whose favors I have enjoyed are 'perverted'?"

"It might be more productive," said Dr. Darvell, "to speak in terms of alternative modes of sexuality rather than ethical categories."

"Our embraces can bestow only death," Sir Francis declared in a sepulchral tone.

"I wouldn't go that far," the black man said. "In certain circumstances, mutual pleasure can be achieved."

"I've tried often enough," Collins said with a sardonic smile. "My appeal diminishes when I reach the point of inviting the lady to share my coffin."

Nick burst out laughing. "No wonder you aren't getting anywhere with a cure, hung up on that fetishistic crap. You're a fossil!"

"Please, no name-calling," the doctor said. "Discuss the behavior, not the person. Now, perhaps we might address the subject of photophobia. A problem you don't have, for example." He glanced at the one patient who hadn't spoken. He looked like a teenage boy, whose skin glittered faintly where the room's overhead light shone on it.

"No, my main problems are romantic, too. I agree that getting involved with mortals can be dangerous. Having been turned at such a young age makes things worse. How would you like to spend an eternity in high school?"

Dr. Darvell asked dryly, "Haven't you considered claiming to be home-schooled?" The door creaked open. "Ah, this must be the remaining member of our group."

A small man with a monocle, a beak-like nose, and a purple-lined cape swooped in. "Greetings!" he intoned. "Please forgive my tardiness and accept my thanks for the invitation to join you. They call me the Count. Do you know *why* they call me the Count? Because I have an irresistible obsessive-compulsive drive to *count things*."

The End

The original version of this story was first published in The Vampire's Crypt 10 (Fall 1994). If you'd like to become better acquainted with Dr. Roger Darvell, he's introduced in Dark Changeling and Child of Twilight, which have been combined in a Kindle edition titled Twilight's Changelings: http://www.tinyurl.com/TwilightsChangelings. Please explore love among the monsters at Carter's Crypt: http://www.margaretlcarter.com

Bow Down by Marc Shapiro

She fell to her knees when she saw me coming
Bowed her head
Clasped her hands in prayer
I walked by
The woman got up and raced away
She would do that every time she saw me
I didn't get it
Did she think I was God
Or Satan
Or worse
If she knew me
It might have been worse
Because it was getting dark
And soon I would fly

Night Gallery

Sunken Treasure: Lost Worlds

Review by the late Tom Johnson

- Title: Sunken Treasure: Lost Worlds
- Author: Hep Aldridge
- Genre: Adventure/Mystery/Action
- Publisher: Budy Media
- ISBN: 978-1083049780
- $15.99 (Paperback); $4.99 (Kindle); 308 pages
- Available at: Amazon, Alibris, Thriftbooks.com, and other retailers
- Rating: 5 Stars

"Adrenalin-pumping Excitement"

Risky Business, LTD is a company formed by a group of friends seeking adventure. They are interested in a fleet of ships that went down in 1715 and may contain sunken treasure. Dr. Colton X. Burnett leads the team, but all are well trained and tough. From the start, the story kicks off with excitement and never lets up. The trail will lead them to two continents, and they may encounter more than they bargained for in their search for a lost civilization.

I was given a copy of the book for an honest review. Readers will find this story filled with thrilling adventure and lots of gunfights and explosions. The adrenalin- pumping excitement will keep you turning the pages. Highly recommended.

Tom Johnson, author of *The Man in the Black Fedora*

The Method

Review by the late Tom Johnson

- Title: The Method
- Author: Jerry Bader
- Genre: Graphic Novel, Crime Noir
- Publisher: MRPwebmedia
- ISBN: 978-0994069818
- Cost: $19.99 (Paperback); $15.99 (Kindle); 132 Pages
- Available at: Amazon, Waterstones, Booktopia, and other retailers
- Rating: 4 Stars

"A New Experience in Graphics."

An unnamed actor down on his luck falls even farther under when his wife leaves him for his agent and depletes his bank account on the way out. With a hundred dollars left in his wallet, he heads for a bar to get drunk. But a strange encounter changes his life suddenly. The waitresses mistake him for someone else, and within minutes, that someone walks into the bar. He's mobster Arnie

Barnardo, the right-hand man of gangster, Carmine, and is a twin to the actor. Becoming drinking partners, they're both drunk when the mobster offers to drive the actor home. On the way, there's an accident, and one is killed, the other is left with amnesia. In the hospital, the survivor meets mob enforcer, Vito, and Arnie's moll, Lonnie. The survivor quickly understands that he'd better play along, or the mob will kill him if he's really the actor.

This was certainly a new experience for me. I was sent the iPad version, which included the audio. Unfortunately, I had trouble with the audio. Either I listened to just the audio, without changing pages, or I lost the audio by changing pages. Every three or four pages, the audio hook-up would return, but just for that page. Although this is a graphic novel with pictures and text, it is also adult in nature, and not meant for youngsters. The "f" bomb is constantly used in dialogue, so anyone offended by language should be aware of the content. The story itself was interesting, though it contained numerous typos; "were" was usually "where," etc. Recommended for adult readers with an interest in crime noir and Graphic Novels with an edge.

Tom Johnson, *Detective Mystery Stories*

Murder: Take Three

Review by the Late Tom Johnson

- ➢ Title: Murder: Take Three
- ➢ Author: April Kelly & Marsha Lyons
- ➢ Genre: Murder Mystery
- ➢ ISBN: 978-0615555065
- ➢ Publisher: Flight Risk Books www.flightriskbooks.com
- ➢ Cost: $10.72; 304 Pages
- ➢ Available at: Amazon, Barnes & Noble, Google Books, and other retailers
- ➢ Rating: 5 Stars

"Just Keeps Getting Better!"

Receiving a big paycheck for proving movie action hero Micah Deifenschlictor did not kill his agent, Blake and Maureen feel good about their investigation until things start looking funny. Another man is arrested after clues lead to him. Now, they're wondering if maybe the clues were planted, and they were supposed to find Micah innocent when in truth, he was the killer.

Micah had served a tour in the Marines, and his bodybuilder's muscles were perfect for action parts, even if he couldn't act. When he left the marines, he brought many of his old military buddies back with him, setting them up in his movies. But is Micah really in charge? Drugs are liquefying his brain, and he doesn't seem to have the intelligence to plan a murder. Blake and Maureen start looking at his movie studio, where ex-marines are patrolling the grounds armed to the teeth. And when Pinnacle Studios notices their interest, Blake's home is burned down, and the suspected body of his wife is found in the ashes, sending Blake temporarily over the edge. However, Maureen remains on the case and discovers that Blake's wife may be alive, and the body was someone else.

Wow! This series just keeps getting better. The characters continue to grow, though the mood becomes a bit darker as Blake and Maureen are pulled deeper into the cases they investigate. There is little mystery to the stories, as the reader understands the set up from the beginning. Still, we get to see the main characters work out their investigation, discovering clues that will lead them to the guilty party. This brings the reader closer to the characters involved. And it is the characters that make the series. The sleazy Hollywood setting is another plus. Highly recommended for mystery buffs who love a good yarn.

Tom Johnson, *Detective Mystery Stories*

The Eye Stone

Review by the late Tom Johnson

- ➢ Title: The Eye Stone
- ➢ Author: Roberto Tiranoschi
- ➢ Genre: Historical Mystery
- ➢ ISBN: 978-1609452650
- ➢ Publisher: Europa Editions
- ➢ Cost: $17.00; 288 pages
- ➢ Available at: Amazon, Barnes & Noble, Kobo, and other retailers
- ➢ Rating: 5 stars

"A Novel of Venice"

Edgardo, a young cleric, deformed at birth and now going blind, seeks a miracle. A miracle to restore his eyesight in order to copy great manuscripts. It's the early Twelfth Century, and the church refuses to accept anything new, believing it will not be from God. Yet there is a rumor that manuscripts exist in the archives of a church library that might hold the key to discovering sight once more. Edgardo travels to Venice, where glassmakers seek great discoveries in their field of art also.

However, Edgardo discovers something else is going on when he arrives. Red-algae is filling the lagoon, and babies and animals are born deformed. To add to the mystery, someone is killing glassmaker apprentices, removing their eyes, and replacing the eyes with colored glass marbles. And the cleric falls in love with a slave, which will lead him away from the church.

Although the story moves slowly, the reader is pulled into the deep mystery, and the characters keep you turning the pages. The historical aspect of early glass making is done in an interesting way, not at all distracting from the story; in fact, it is embedded into the mystery in a way that adds purpose to the overall storytelling. This may not be for readers of fast action, but fans of mystery lovers will find it a good read, as well as having a strong twist at the end. I'm not sure how accurate the historical Venice is, but the mystery is certainly good. Highly recommended.

Tom Johnson, *Detective Mystery Stories*

Shadow of the Dagger

Review by the late Tom Johnson

- ➢ Title: Shadow of The Dagger
- ➢ Author: Anne Greene
- ➢ Genre: Christian/Romance/Thriller
- ➢ Publisher: Elk Lake Publishing
- ➢ ISBN: 978-1951080204
- ➢ Cost: $12.99 (Paperback); $2.99 (Kindle); 400 pages
- ➢ Available at: Amazon, Barnes & Noble, Google Books, and other retailers
- ➢ Rating: 5 Stars

We meet Nicole Phillips when she travels to the crash site of the plane piloted by her husband. There was no body, but investigators believe coyotes may have dragged the body away. A year later, her brother is invited to an archeological dig in Turkey, and he talks Nicole into joining him. Unfortunately, when she arrives in Turkey, she discovers Ian has been kidnapped. In the meantime, CIA analyst Josh Baruch believes the man who killed his brother is responsible for the kidnapping and is waiting in Turkey for Nicole Phillips when she arrives, as he plans on using her for bait to catch Helmut Meier, better known as The Viper, and the murderer of Josh's brother.

The author sent me a copy of the book for an honest review. This is a complicated plot, with interesting characters, set in a location known for international spies and intrigue. Josh Baruch is a Jewish American, and well familiar with Turkey, as he was stationed at Incirlik AFB in Adana, Turkey, a place that I also know well. I was stationed there with the Army in 1964, at TUSLOG, as a squad leader with the rank of corporal.

This was a great read, though a few things did bother me. The villain is supposedly the third richest man in the world but seems to be after small profit in current crime, and a man so rich should have enough lawyers to keep him out of jail (in this case, an American federal prison). Plus, we find that there is someone pulling his strings also, a minor criminal behind the whole mess, and he is after Nicole Phillips and the treasure. Now for detective Pavlik, a Russian with the Turkey police, and master of disguise who plays many parts that just don't seem to fit. In the end, an American Air Force rescue team saves the day on Turkey soil, which also was a worrisome finale to a great plot. Personally, it would have appeared more legit if the team was led by a Turkey command. Overall, the Christian background is a delight in this international thriller set in Muslim-controlled Turkey and well worth the read. Highly recommended.

Tom Johnson, Author of *The Man in the Black Fedora*

Oklahoma Winds

Review by the late Tom Johnson

- Title: Oklahoma Winds (A Sydney St. John Mystery #1)
- Author: Cary Osborne
- Genre: Cozy Mystery
- Publisher: Crossroad Press
- ISBN # 978-1941408704
- Cost: $12.99 (Paperback); $2.99 (Kindle); 194 Pages
- Available at: Amazon, Kobo Books, Google Books, and other retailers
- Rating: 4 Stars

Sydney St. John is the archivist for records in Gansel, Oklahoma. It's May of the present day and tornado season. Everyone is watching the weather for violent storms. Arriving at work one morning, she finds her university intern dead. Sydney believes her murder involves the latest material donated to the archives. While the local and state police investigate the homicide, she concentrates on the material, believing the answers lie there.

In 1938, Josiah Bartlett was a filmmaker that traveled to small towns, making short films using local children. In Vernon, he wrote a play that involved a young 12-year-old girl being kidnapped, and two young boys rescue her from an old barn. But something goes wrong. The girl, Violet Parsons, really disappears. At the same time, a banker is reported kidnapped, and a ransom of two hundred thousand dollars is asked for his return. The money was paid, but his body was later found. Sydney follows the clues in the archives and films. A story ~~slowly~~ unravels, making her believe that Violet Parsons is still alive, but using another name, and may have been involved in the murder of the banker. But complications arise when Josiah's grandson, Ben Bartlett, comes from California to look through the material. Sydney's afraid she may be falling for him, and he could be the murderer. Mixed with the danger of a killer loose in Gansel, there are severe storms and tornados that make life difficult in the area.

I was given a copy of the book for an honest review. This was an interesting plot, and I wanted to find out the truth about the missing girl in 1938, but like most cozy mysteries, the story moves slowly, even with the storms and attempts on Sydney's life. The story is clean, and sex is kept in the background. Highly recommended.

Tom Johnson, Author of *Those Alien Skies*

Astounding

Review by the late Tom Johnson

- Title: Astounding
- Author: Alec Nebala-Lee
- Genre: SF/Biography
- Publisher: Dey Street Books
- ISBN: 978-0062571946
- Cost: $16.50 (hardback); $13.39 (Paperback); 544 Pages
- Available at: Amazon, Barnes & Noble, Google Books, and other retailers
- Rating: 5 Stars

"A Monument to the Past"

Astounding was the leading science fiction magazine in the Golden Age of SF. When John Campbell took over editorial control, the stories became more believable than the previous soap opera appearing in the news rack magazines of the day. The authors submitting to *Astounding* knew that their stories better show real science and nuts and bolts technology if they wanted to be published in John Campbell's magazine. Three such authors were Isaac Asimov, Robert A. Heinlein, and L. Ron Hubbard. This book covers them and John Campbell in biographies that dig into their backgrounds, showing not only their talents but also their faults. It also looks at the women behind the men. It's a history that looks into the magazine in that period when *Astounding* led the field.

I was captivated by the stories I heard about these men and women. As a young reader in the early 1950s, I discovered *Astounding* and the other SF magazines, and read the likes of A.E. van Vogt, Ray Bradbury, George O. Smith, and the rest. For those of you who want to learn more about *Astounding* and the Golden Age of science fiction and the authors, I highly recommend this book.

Tom Johnson, Author of *Worlds of Tomorrow*

Haunted Charlottesville

Review by the late Tom Johnson

- ➢ Title: Haunted Charlottesville and Surrounding Counties
- ➢ Author: Susan Schwartz
- ➢ Genre: Paranormal
- ➢ Publisher: Schiffer Publishing
- ➢ ISBN: 978-0764357556
- ➢ Cost: $18.99 (Paperback); 196 pages
- ➢ Available at: Amazon, Barnes & Noble, Target, and other retailers
- ➢ Rating: 5 Stars

"A Look at Haunted Places in Virginia"

In Charlottesville and the surrounding counties, a number of places and buildings appear to be haunted. The author and her brother tour the wide area, she looking for signs and stories of hauntings, and her brother taking pictures of the places they visit. Most hauntings appear to be connected to battles of the Civil War that took place in this area of Virginia, but there are murders that also tend to have ghostly apparitions, as well.

Reading about the hauntings was fun, though in my opinion, they are not restless souls that haven't crossed over yet, but the evil reflections of violent death and murder that remain in those areas, leaving a passageway for demons to emerge. I also love great architect, and the photographs of the mansions and homes where these hauntings took place are beautifully displayed throughout the narrative.

War is violent and evil, and if we learned anything from the Civil War, brother should not fight brother again. There are other ways to achieve peace without massive killing of one another. Regardless of your opinion of ghosts and phantoms, this book will hold your interest to the last page. Highly recommended.

Tom Johnson, Author of *Carnival of Death*

Spooky Tutti Frutti

Review by Keily Blair

- ➢ Title: Spooky Tutti Frutti
- ➢ Author: Margaret L. Carter
- ➢ Genre: Fantasy Romance
- ➢ Publisher: The Wild Rose Press, Inc. (www.thewildrosepress.com)
- ➢ ISBN: 978-1509231683
- ➢ Price: $0.99; 38 pages
- ➢ Available at: Amazon, Barnes & Noble, Scribd, Google Books, Kobo, and Apple Books
- ➢ Rating: 5 Stars

Celia Rossi is in search of temporary help and a new ice cream flavor for her ice cream parlor. She is eager to boost sales at the weekend boat race and prove that her business isn't a financial "black hole." Suddenly, the enigmatic Suzie appears in her shop with a passion for creating the perfect tutti frutti ice cream. The two make the perfect team as they try different recipes, but Celia can't help but find Suzie's random disappearances a little strange. Suzie grows more and more frustrated as she searches for her own lost recipe, and Celia finds herself pulled into the girl's paranormal quest to fulfill a wish from long ago.

The greatest strength of this story lies in its detail. Carter brings mouthwatering ice cream and the interior of a 50s style ice cream parlor to life. She drops little details that you could just skim over if you're reading too fast, but I guarantee you'll want to savor this read. Carter has created the perfect blend of delicious paranormal mystery, fantasy romance, and light-hearted summer fun as sweet as tutti frutti ice cream.

The Great Hall of Ahkurst
by
Lee Clark Zumpe

Tarak limped along the long corridor, muttering to himself beneath the flickering fluorescents. The subterranean passage stretched out before and behind him, a serpentine artery curving beneath the surface of the planet. Once bright and full of life, the grimy channel had fallen into disrepair and contemptible neglect over the years. A wave of systems failures, a spate of irreparable malfunctions, and a generation of mechanically inept slackers had sealed the lid on this coffin.

Tarak knew this place would be his tomb. The underlings would eventually find a way through the network of sensors and automated battle stations, overrun the passages, and kill anyone they found. The underlings would have their revenge upon him if age itself did not lay claim to him first.

The old man cursed the fate that had befallen his beloved home.

Tarak tugged at his mangy beard. His great-great-great grandfather had worked on this very corridor, sweating in the grim darkness and chipping away at the stone with his pickaxe. As a boy, Tarak had heard stories dating back hundreds of years – stories retold generation after generation by his family, over tea, after dinner. His grandfather spoke of the wars his ancestors fought to claim their empire and of the horrors they found deep in the earth.

Tarak caressed the steel buttress with a trembling hand. His pudgy fingers tapped the reinforcements, taunting them to admit the weakness of their age. Behind the thick metal casing, beneath that veil of fortification, the solid rock of the earth's crust bristled with hideous life.

Tarak wondered how much longer these walls would stand.

> Weakest of all are those castle walls
> Guarding nothing but shadowy halls.

An old proverb, one Tarak remembered from childhood. No one read the scriptures any more, of course, but those verses had a way of surfacing at appropriate moments to unsettle the soul.

Tarak opted to remain behind when most of his kind chose to forsake the realm. Only a handful remained now, wandering the lonely passages, dreaming about past glories and reliving ancient battles through song and story. Old men like Tarak – too stubborn or too proud to relinquish their heritage – now haunted these halls, breathing the last few breaths of musty air in their lost world.

Tired and cheerless, the little old man propped his stubby bones against the wall, pressing his furrowed brow against the cold steel plates. He had been old when lasers had replaced swords, when drills had replaced shovels, and when antibacterial ointments had replaced folk remedies. He had watched as the handwritten tomes of his ancestors had been digitized and stored on computers. He had watched as the crude artificial intelligence of machines had been substituted for soldiers along the watchtowers. Like a creeping tumor, technology had eclipsed everything that had been, had swallowed his birthright, and had devalued the legacy of his people.

Technology had even seduced his children away from him, into different lives on another world.

A faint whisper echoed through the corridor. Behind him, the shadows writhed. The old man shuddered and picked up his pace.

The corridor soon gave way to a vast enclosure – the Great Hall of Ahkurst. Tarak immediately felt soothed by the warmth of torchlight. The sparkling glow of the flames illuminated the hall, peeling back the shadows to reveal the magnificent painting spread across the ceiling. The fresco recorded the history of his race from the time they had been driven underground. It depicted the most renowned of their leaders, revealed the most triumphant scenes of their wars with the underlings, and chronicled the slow but steady progress of their empire.

No more than a dozen Elders sat at the Long Table. Tarak recognized Aziz and Ezra, the brothers from Tahlmot Bottoms. On his right hand sat Luranius of Toth. On his left, he found Bohr.

"Tarak, old friend – it is good to see you." Urik, a decorated warrior in his youth, nodded and smiled. "We were just speaking of the Kobalds. Have you seen any?"

"No … but," Tarak took a seat at the table, glancing over his shoulder. He could not shake the feeling that something had followed him. "Something is out there. Something must be out there. The halls aren't as still as they once were."

"Aye," chimed in Aziz. "And something smells out there."

"That's probably Ezra's feet!" Luranius retained the worst qualities of his ancestors. He chuckled though no one else found his witticisms particularly funny.

The Elders spoke of Kobolds encroaching on the outermost perimeters. They spoke of disappearances amongst the residents of the outlying communities – the small, unshielded villages whose inhabitants shunned all forms of technology. Their numbers had been in decline for some time, but now reports suggested only a few dozen remained.

"It's the Kobalds, it must be," Ezra barked. "They've always been just outside of our walls, waiting for an opportunity." Coal-black and mindless, the Kobolds lumbered through the darkest hollows of the world. Legends claimed they feasted on solid rock and drank lava like water. "They've come to reclaim the territory they lost in the wars…"

"And if they have … how long before the other underlings become their allies? How long before the rock wraiths and the orcs and the dragons stir from their nests?" Tarak accepted a goblet of ale offered to him by a servant. "How long before we are faced with more formidable threats than those bumbling oafs?"

"We have sufficient weapons to…"

"Sufficient weapons? Our laser cannons have no energy to power them. Our plasma rifles are scattered across hundreds of miles of tunnels, gathering dust in storerooms and closets and kitchen pantries. Our dilapidated android sentries all short-circuited years ago." Tarak wrestled his dagger free from its sheath and thrust it into the stale air of the room. "This is the only weapon I trust…"

Even as Tarak's words echoed through the hall, an exceptional blast of wind flooded the chamber, extinguishing all but one of the torchlights. Formerly managed by mechanized climate control mainframes, such uncontrolled currents of air had become more and more common.

"Can't someone look into that blasted weather system?" Luranius tugged at his cloak, pulling it close to his stout body. He folded his stubby arms across his chest, hid his shaking hands beneath the material. The cold bothered his thick, stunted bones. "Perhaps we should have joined the others. Perhaps we should have given in and left all this behind."

"No…" Bohr, who had been silent until now, spoke. "I do not blame those who migrated – this is a dying world to them, and they had whole lifetimes before them. But for us – for the Elders – we would not fit in well with the surface-dwellers."

"We could have, had we chosen to," Luranius reminded him. "The DNA restructuring procedure would have given us the appearance of the surface-dwellers…"

"Aye," said Bohr, "But we would never be surface-dwellers." Bohr's face crumpled into shadowy ridges as he fought back emotion. His three daughters had gone to live on the surface, and the old man missed them. "Those who left were of a different generation – they accepted the marvelous gifts of science and technology without question, without hesitation. We prefer the old ways. Though some of the comforts of the modern age appeal to us, we still favor to live our lives as our ancestors lived theirs." Bohr smiled as he tilted his head back and eyed the painting overhead, now barely discernible in the thickening shadows. "I don't know about the rest of you, but I also prefer to die here with my ancestors – nestled in the warm earth, and not upon some roofless, grassy pasture beneath endless skies where beasts can ravage my lifeless corpse."

Silence fell upon the room as each of the Elders nodded in agreement. Unlike their children, the Elders remained shackled to the customs and traditions of their forebears.

"Enough of these shadows. Let us have some light again," Luranius said.

Aziz and Ezra took leave of their comfortable chairs and began relighting the firebrands.

"Wait," Tarak said, turning and peering down the corridor that had delivered him to the Great Hall. He sniffed at the still fluctuating stream of air. "Do you smell that?"

The Kobalds shambled out of the shadows like a slow-moving rockslide, their stony pitch-black hides interrupted only by the crimson fire of their eyes. The dark, dim-witted things howled as they approached their ancient enemies.

"*Breach!*" screamed Luranius, and he leapt to his feet and scampered across the Great Hall to the far end of the room.

Tarak jumped up onto the face of the table, brandishing his blade with no less courage than his ancestors had in the wars of old. Urik stood by his side, a laser pistol gripped firmly in his hand.

"Does that thing work?" Tarak snarled out of the corner of his mouth, never once taking his eyes off the loathsome Kobalds.

"It used to…haven't had any reason to use it in a hundred years."

"Aziz, Ezra!" Tarak and Urik edged across the table until they stood in the center. Tarak spun his head around, scanning the shadows. "Where are you two? Find something to defend yourselves with and get up here!"

"They left." One of the Kobalds hobbled over to Tarak's chair and sat down in it. "Looks like you two," the Kobald sputtered, "Have been left to defend the realm on your own…"

"You…you speak?" Tarak's eyes had grown wide with astonishment. Nothing in the history of his people had indicated Kobalds had the capacity for intelligent dialogue. "What…what do you want?"

"Well," the Kobald said, "An apology would be nice, but, short of that, we'd like to reclaim some of our property taken by your ancestors."

"But we…"

"Look, you don't need it, and there's hardly any of you left." The Kobald extended an arm and clasped Tarak's goblet of ale. He drew it to his lips and sipped at it. From the expression on his gritty face, he appeared to be pleased with the taste. "We've gotten tired of living in caverns, sleeping on rocks. We'd like to fill in some of your vacant lodgings."

"You want to live with us?"

"Why not? We'd like to learn more about how you built this place." The Kobald smiled, its crimson eyes narrowing into narrow slits. "It would be fair compensation for what your ancestors did to mine, don't you think?"

"I suppose…" Tarak gradually lowered his dagger. Urik, standing beside him, scratched his head.

"Maybe we could even help you get some of your equipment working again – seems like things have started to fall apart around here."

"Maybe…"

"I know all this is rather sudden, and I'm sure you need to discuss things with your governing council." The Kobald stood, bowing in respect. "We will take our leave now, and we will give you some time to think things over."

"Fine…"

"Our attaché will be in contact with you to negotiate a settlement." Moving at a snail's pace, the band of Kobalds filed back into the corridor. "It's been a pleasure meeting you."

Moments later, Tarak and Urik still stood shaking on the long table beneath the vast painting in the middle of the Great Hall of Ahkurst. The other Elders had apparently scattered throughout the network of tunnels and probably cowered in the shadows awaiting gruesome and violent deaths.

Tarak sheathed his dagger and sat down on the edge of the table.

"So much for the glory of battle," Tarak mused.

"It's a strange, new world," Urik admitted, sitting down beside his friend. "Do you think the dragons have ambassadors and mediators, too?"

The End

Beyond the Reaches of Dawn by Lee Clark Zumpe

Stone-faced Death
prattles on endlessly
about quotas and loopholes
and appeals and the like;
I never much cared for your brother.

Sleep, your bratty little spawn,
wanders around the crowd,
tugging at coattails
till he curls up at the foot of the stairs;
Isn't it past that boy's bedtime?

Ah, but you: You are the queen,
The empress of this gala affair.
None could be so delicate, so fair,
So welcoming as you, my dear.
Beautiful Night, may I have this dance?

Lianne
by
Linda Barrett

One:

When I opened the door of the Raden, the temple of the good luck goddess, Bree-Ahm, my nose picked up the smell of some freaky oil. It gave off this odor of sweet, musty flowers. It started me coughing and gagging for air in this stone dive. My canine-human mutant nose is ten times stronger than a regular person's. That's why I became a private investigator.

"Watch out for the glass!" the girl shouted, her soft, sweet voice echoing in the Raden's wide stone halls.

I looked down to see millions of glass shards glittering in front of me. I drew one foot back because I had flip flops on.

As I looked up at this crazy place, my eyes scanned everything. Stone statues carved in the columns along the walls surrounded the altar. Someone must have spent years on this place of worship. Wooden benches, stone statues, and even gold went into the making of this place. Even the incense smelled ritzy.

The guards in their black leather tunics reminded me of some 1980s sci-fi movie with Mel Gibson in it. They bared their arms and legs and wore metal spikes on their breast plates. I smelled sweat and cigarette smoke on their bodies. The girl guard towered over me. She looked too cute to be working with these moonlighting professional wrestlers.

She aimed a spear at me, her eyes doing the same thing. I saw a little tuft of red hair coming out of her helmet.

"Hi, I'm Sophia Wisenheimer." I laughed, waving feebly at her. "I came here to find the girl,"

The foxlike girl aimed her eyes and her spear at me.

"The Vestal?" she brayed in a Southern accent.

"Ah-yeah!" I laughed. "I got a telephone call from a friend. She said that she needed my help!"

"Telephone call?" the girl asked.

"Ah-yeah, she called me up at seven in the evening. Spoke with a very strange accent. She caught me in the middle of *Bowling for Food*."

"Bowling for Food?" she asked. Her gray eyes blanked.

"I watch it every night at seven, just after the network news."

"News?"

"*Bowling for Food* is a game show. People bowl against each other to win a week's worth of groceries. It's the hottest show on TV. It's lotsa laughs."

"TV?"

"Yeah, television."

"Telephone?"

"You use it to call people. It's this device, and it's got wires and-"

The guard aimed her spear at me. "Outworlder!" she shouted.

"Actually, I'm a private investigator. It's like my second job. I mean my second case. Just before I get my license. I-um-look for missing people. Your friend said to come here and find the vestal—"My body shook at the spear pointed in my black and pink nose.

"Lianne," the guard turned and faced another one with a black eye patch on his left eye. The black patched eye guy turned to me.

"She the vestal who escaped," he said in a dead voice.

Two

My legs shook as I stood before the high priest in this long, stone room. Something scared me about him. When I looked into his eyes, I felt sharp pain in the middle of my head. His beefy face had a gray complexion around his cheeks.

"Ah, Frauline Weisenheimer!" he purred as he looked down at me from his crude stone chair. He looked like a piece of dead meat that was left in the refrigerator for a few months. His odor sure smelled like it, too.

"The huma-animal private investigator. It is so good to see you."

"You're ... uh," His name spoke to me in the center of my head.

"Ian Hand, high priest of Uudah, a suburb of Stockton, California. We have need of your services," his thoughts purred into mine.

I felt my heart shaking in my chest. The weird feeling in the middle of my head still forced me to look into his gray marble eyes.

My mouth felt like a wind-up toy when I spoke.

"Ah, good to see you, too," I stammered. How the heck did he know my name? I didn't even open my mouth.

"Frauline Weisenheimer, I read about your fame from the *Ambler Gazette* a few months ago," he purred.

"Ah, it got me kicked out of there!" I laughed.

He waved a hand at me. Even that looked like a piece of rotting meat!

"Lianne Weaver Kennedy was a fine vestal. Her mother, Amethyst Blake was a fine psychic."

"She died. Someone in London found her about ... seven years ago ... in some kind of...," I shuddered at the memory of the woman's brutal death. The English press love to report the bloody, gory details of even making steak and kidney pie with Yorkshire Pudding in their Food section.

Ian Hand brought his hands together and bowed at the waist.

"Ah, a tragedy if there ever was one!" He sighed, but his voice remained somewhat happy. Now, that scared me even more.

"And how is Eddie Puss Rex?" he rose and stared at me.

"He's on top of the world now." I fudged around and waved my hand.

"Especially after you chased him up that tree. How comical! A canine-human hybrid detective chasing a feline-human hybrid psychic up a large pine tree in your town's community park." His body bounced from laughter.

"Ah, let's get back into the runaway vestal, please?" I stammered.

He looked like Buddha as he sat there on the throne in his lotus position. His inner quarters also gave me chills. Gargoyle-faced statues glared down with opened mouths ready to eat me whole. I couldn't help but look at them while that joker talked on and on. I worried that one of those creepy things would turn on me.

"Frauline Weisenheimer." He sighed. "I want you to find Lianne Weaver Kennedy. She is crucial for the upcoming feast of Bree-Ahm. If she is not present, Uudah will not experience good luck for the coming year. A vestal like she dedicated to the goddess Bree-Ahm's service is important in the good luck ritual."

I stared back at him.

"Ah, yeah." I said, hiding the fact he confused me.

Three

After rolling up my pink Princess Diana British Union pound notes to store them in my wrist pouch, I went to bed in a trailer park not too far from Uudah. I closed my eyes to see Lord Hand smirking back at me. That sight of that horrible lumpy gray face made me open them real wide. That soft spoken voiced weirdo made me too scared to sleep.

This Uudah place always gave me the willies. Whenever I passed through it, this bad smell used to get into my nose and make me cough. Its people made me think of those "Mad Max" movies. Nobody had cars or antennas or any other modern thing like the rest of Northern California. People wore rags and drove ox carts. Little farm plots and rickety houses surrounded huge stone mansions. The crude, scary statues on every corner of that town always stared me in the face.

Under my Mickey Mouse flashlight, I studied Lianne's picture. They didn't have photographs, but they did have paintings. Some artsy type painted this beautiful young girl on a piece of something. They did a great job on it, too.

She must've been a big, husky thing with wavy light brown hair that fell over the corner of her eye. Her pink rose petal lips smirked at you in a seductive manner. She wore a solid gold bikini with huge orange and red gems on it. Maybe she was Lord Hand's girlfriend who didn't like the big gray guy anyway. She probably ran off to find some barbarian swordsman.

"What the heck's a vestal?" I wondered.

I spent the whole night with the light on, my bed shaking under me. It wasn't demonic possession but my fear of Uudah's demons.

Four

When the morning came, I hurried over to the pay phone to call Sunshine Smith, my Ambler, Pennsylvania landlady. She answered the phone with her pleasant-sounding belch. I told her about the sleepless night I spent in the Uudah, California trailer park.

"Whattya so afraid of?" Sunshine shouted at me from the payphone. Her cawing comforted me even from Ambler, Pennsylvania. "Those cultists don't scare me. You're a fraidy dog-human."

"This place's spook central!" I whined, clutching my bathrobe.

"Some private eye you are!" she sneered. "Look at you. Wearing a Minnie Mouse pajama set. Do you think Jim Rockford wore such stuff?"

Sunshine's husband, Alan, took the phone.

"Hey! Puppy!" he called. "How's Sherlock Bones?"

"I need a Watson. I gotta find someone who will keep me sane," I cried, grasping at the telephone.

"Alan," Sunshine whispered on the other end. "Don't let her make you feel sorry for her...,"

"Shut up, you cow!" Alan sneered.

"Alan! Don't give into her. She's an idiot. Who in their right mind would hire a P.I. who had a Little Mermaid night light?"

"Keep outta this! I put up with your thong underwear when you were 60 years old," Alan said.

"Oh yeah?" Sunshine shouted. "What about you and that Mohawk? Why does a 75-year-old man wear a Mohawk?"

"It makes me look younger." Alan growled.

"It makes you look stupid!" She spat.

"You're 73, and you *still* have a navel ring. Now, that's stupid!" he yelled.

Just as they started another argument, I hung up the phone and wiped my eyes. They really loved each other.

As I left the telephone booth, I came face to face with a black-cloaked shadow. It stood before the booth's entrance.

"I knew you were here. You are the one searching for me. Your name is Sophia. Sophia, the canine human investigator. Am I right?"

The black shadow moved its seductively full lips in a chillingly familiar voice.

Five

I recognized her voice from a week ago from the Hatboro YMCA's telephone. I set up living quarters there the day after Ambler's mayor kicked me out. That sexy-voiced person saw my number someplace. She called, saying she needed my help. I kept wondering where she called me since Uudah in Northern California had no telephones, no cars, no whatever. Their cult pulled the town back into the Stone Age.

Her voice floated from the black cloak. I only heard the soft scuffle of her feet. That perfume made me cough again.

"Who is this?" I gasped for air.

Pulling off her hood, she revealed her deep gold hair that curved around her face. Earrings with ice cube-big gems hung from her ears. Her voice sounded just as sexy as her face. Glittering green eyes stared back at me. Her rosebud mouth stood straight.

"I am Lianne Weaver Kennedy. I escaped from the Raden Temple of Bree-Am, the Goddess of Good Fortune."

"So," I stammered, "you're her. They're paying me a quite a lot of rocks for your return."

"You must help me," she breathed, "I am in great danger."

I laughed. How could I help her?

"Where the heck have you been?" I stammered, "Your boyfriend is waiting for you to return. Didn't you run off with Conan, the Barbarian? You have to come back. He's looking for you. He can't start the festival without you. You're the star!"

Her eyes half-closed. She said nothing, as if measuring her words.

"I have seen you in my thoughts. My mother had the same power," she said.

I grasped at my cross. "Ma'am! Now, you're scaring me. I don't dig that psychic stuff. Not what it did to...,"

"You ran to another god who took the power away. Why?" she asked.

"Let's get down to my business. Your rotting meat-smelling sugar daddy wants you back. You're a good luck symbol to Uudah's people....," I began.

She moved closer. The moonlight shone on her huge, hanging earrings. The woman must've had pretty strong earlobes to hold those things up. I stared at a brief flash of a jeweled bikini.

"I am a marked woman," she began.

"I'm scared to death of this place. Everyone can read my mind around here. Everybody worships ugly stone statues. This place needs a few good-"

"Missionaries?" she finished.

"You betcha!" I spat.

"It is impossible for your god to enter here. The darkness of many souls rests here," she said.

"Nothing's impossible with God." I barked. Retreating back to the phone booth, I shut the

60

door against her curvaceous form. She reached out and touched it with elegant hands. Her finger-nails glittered as fancy as stained glass windows.

"Your God can save me. He brought you here, did He not?"

"You're a … a Pagan! What do you know of my-my-my God?"

"Ian Hand plans to kill me," she whispered.

I stopped to think on this. No wonder I found that guy so creepy!

"Hey," I sputtered. "I've saved a life before. I can do it again. Whattya want me to do?"

Six

"You carry the symbol of your god," she said, studying my crucifix.

"He's an awesome God. He won't let ya down." I joyfully gasped.

Her clear green eyes studied mine. They narrowed as if concentrating on my mind.

"Why would he kill you?" I asked, staring in the booth at her.

"I am selected to die for the goddess Bree-Ahm," she replied.

"What's that?"

"She brings good fortune. A virgin sacrifice is what she requires,"

"Ah, they never taught me that at Oxford."

She pulled off her cloak to show off her lush body. Orange and red gemstones glittered from the gold plates around her curves.

"It must feel heavy on you. Don't wear that in San Francisco, either. Those pickpockets will chase you for blocks. I don't get the thing about you wearing all that jewelry. Can't they just melt down the gold and sell them gems to feed their people? A solid gold bikini's too much loot to wear around," I said.

"You do not understand our ways. Their gods scare them as they do you. Ian Hand makes them bow out of fear. He has the black arts under belt!"

"Yep." I shivered. "That's what freaks me out about him! What do we have to do to get him? Pour a bucket of water on him and watch him melt?"

She nodded her head, her hair bouncing around her face.

"I want to leave here before he captures me."

"I gotta take you back to him! He's paying me a lot to bring you back." I shot out my hands.

Suddenly, she whipped out her gun. As I stared down at its shining metal form, I pondered over the fact that someone could carry a piece while wearing only that bikini.

"How'd you get a gun in California?" I shouted, despite the fear pounding in my heart. "It's a Communist state! Guns are illegal. Are you sure you can shoot that thing?" I backed into the phone booth.

"That is not necessary at this time. I am desperate to escape Uudah and return to England."

She moved into the phone booth. Her elegant finger tugged on the gun's trigger.

"Take me into Stockton," she commanded, tilting up her straight nose.

"Okay!" I threw up my hands.

Seven

The people on the Stockton-bound bus gave us strange looks when we boarded. They pulled off their Walkmans and looked up from their gossip magazines as we tried to find a seat in the back. The bus driver turned his head and gave us this "don't give me grief look."

"Wat's dis!" he shouted, his yellow toothpick bobbing in his open mouth. "Where my money?"

I reached into my vest's pocket.

"I gotta TransPass for California!" I shouted before thumbing at the chick in the black cloak. "She's a foreigner. From Uudah in the wine country,"

The driver jerked on his brakes and shut down the bus. His big, barrel shaped body waddled down the aisle towards us. The man's head just grazed the roof. He took over all of the rest of the space with that big, bear body of his. When he aimed a finger at us, his toothpick bounced as he spoke.

"Hey, you gonna sneak that witch in a black cloak on my bus without paying? Not on my route!" he shouted. All those heads turned to see me. Some of them laughed; others lowered their eyebrows and frowned. This would not be a good escape.

Lianne spoke, not daring to take off her cloak and revealed her face.

"I have the money, sir," she said, reaching into her heavy garment. She pulled out her clenched hand from her glittering bra and handed him something. He looked down at it in his palm. He then glanced up at her.

"What is this?" he whined.

"It will be enough to suffice," she purred.

"What'd she say?" He looked at me.

"Ah, she ... um ... has enough..." My eyes widened. Turning to her, I gave her a strange look. What was this freaky chick doing?

The driver looked down at his palm again.

"Damn!" He breathed and put it in his pocket as he went back to his seat and started up the bus again. The bus roared into life, and we started off towards Stockton.

"What the heck did you give him?" I nudged her.

She jerked her head to me.

"It is something that my mother taught me to give in times of crisis," she said in her sexy Masterpiece Theater English.

"It looks like you gave him a big wad of air. He didn't have anything in his hand." I hissed.

"I did give him something ... but in his mind."

Now that remark made me jump even more.

Eight

Stockton, California looked normal on the outside for the moment. I watched subcompacts roll up and down the streets. The trans-fat service stations put their trans-fat gasolines into their trans-fat-operated cars. The bowling alley across the bridge had cars jammed in its parking lot. Al-Farqui Savings Bank's big brown building had a big yellow banner over it that read:

"For Ramadan, we will be closed!"

Buddhist monks in their orange robes walked towards the Dunkin' Donuts in the shopping mall, just across from the Brittany Spears Diner and Grocery King. It still looked like the Stockton, California area that Sunshine showed me on her old I-phone camera.

The bus driver opened the doors and stared at the little piece of nothing in the sunlight before his eyes. He whistled in awe and rubbed this little piece of nothing on his work shirt before holding it up again and squinting at it in the light.

I turned to Lianne.

"Now, how did you do that?" I asked.

She still didn't say a thing when we came to this motel along the street. I panted for miles and miles because of all the walking we did. The sun scorched down upon us. She didn't even care about the black cloak covering her body. Maybe she was right to wear it. You can't go around, wearing that solid gold bikini thing without being robbed for it.

After a while, I fell over onto the motel's entrance.

"Let's take a break!" I gasped.

She pointed a finger at the motel's door.

"It's right there." she said without emotion.

Strange and suspicious characters swarmed around the place. Couples glanced sidelong at us as they made their ways to rooms for their affairs. A few human-animal hybrid creatures stood around, wearing their mange with sleazy pride. They crouched in doorways and skulked on patio chairs. Cigarettes dangled from their half-human, half-animal mouths. I prayed every second that they wouldn't tangle with me or her.

She led me to a room along the far side of the place. I staggered behind her as best as I could.

"How are you going to open the door?" I asked. "You have to go to the manager in the office to get a key."

"Wait," she said in her usual emotionless manner.

The door seemed to open in slow motion. We stood face to face with the interior's brown darkness.

"Enter," a female voice intoned from within. It sounded exactly like Lianne. I turned to stare at her. She only placed her long fingered hand onto my muzzle, indicating that I should shut up.

We came in and my eyes accustomed itself to its surroundings. A cloaked female form arose from an armchair placed before a queen-sized bed. She removed her cloak's hood. I came face to face with an exact Lianne duplicate. They stared at each other in silence. I did a triple take before the blood in my head roared in my tiny lopped ears.

As I fell over onto the carpet, the room faded to pitch black.

Nine

Cold water spilled from my mouth onto my t-shirt. One of the Liannes must've brought me a glass to wake me up. The Lianne sitting on the side of my bed placed my head back onto the pillow and held up the half-full glass. Her eyes studied mine.

The Lianne on the bed turned and spoke back to the other one in it.

"I am sorry," she spoke to me with her Masterpiece Theater accent. "The one who met you at the telephone booth was my love, Sabin. He came in the form of a gorilla and took me away from the Raden. Ian Hand did not tell you that, did he?"

Anger surged through me as I sat up on the bed.

"Look! I need a score card here. Things are happening too fast. First, one of you came to the trailer park and met me at the telephone booth. I take one of you on the bus where you play some magic trick on the bus driver to pay your way over here. We come here, and I see two of you. Ian Hand wants to sacrifice you for his creepy goddess. You call me all the way from Uudah in Northern California to save your life. I come out here and..."

The Lianne standing at the foot of the bed moved back towards the walk-in closet. She grew a foot taller, and her shoulders broadened. Her shining golden eyes narrowed their irises. The feminine curves of her face squared into masculine features. Within seconds, I came face to face with a handsome man. A strong burning smell rose from his body during his transformation.

The Lianne sitting on the bed steadied me with her long-fingered hand as I screamed.

"This is Sabin the Great. He is a shapeshifting jewel thief," she said.

It all came back to me. I fought to hold down the nausea from his intense transformation trick's odor.

"So you're the guy who steals jewels from all over the world," I choked.

The handsome guy nodded. "Yes," he said in his thick accent.

"And when you kidnaped her, you fell in love?" I asked.

He nodded. "Yes," he said again.

I slapped my hand to my tan furry forehead.

"Now I get it! I get it. And now you want to get away from Ian Hand. That creepy, gray guy who wants to sacrifice Lianne. Am I right?"

"Yes!" Lianne and Sabin chorused together.

"Well, what're you two waiting for? You, hunk with the golden eyes and the funny accent. Change into something big with strong wings and take Lianne and me to San Francisco, and we'll pawn off all those jewels and start a new life. Isn't that easy enough?" I shouted.

Sabin the Great stepped forward. His gilded eyebrows shot downward. His demi-godlike features hardened with defiance. "It is not that easy...," he started.

Outside, someone shrieked from the parking lot.

"Look!" the female voice cried. A babble of frightened voices followed her.

"What is that? It's flying overhead!" I heard the whirr of a camera lens. A huge bird cried from the skies, its shriek growing louder as it neared the motel. A chorus of screams and shouts erupted around the area. The unseen picture taker kept popping picture after picture.

"Look at that big, black bird!" A feline-human howled.

"It's coming closer. Madre De Dios!" a Latino hollered.

"It looks like it's gonna take off the roof!" a man shouted.

"Run!" A woman cried.

The bird dug its claws into the roof directly over our room. Lianne pulled me off the bed and shoved me into the bathroom. She pushed me into the bathtub then jumped in with me, drawing the curtain around us.

As the bird's claws tore into the motel's roof and pulled off its foundation, shingles, beams and all, I nearly kissed the bathtub's bottom. Lianne's bosomy body covered mine. She squished me into its smooth surface. A female scream pierced the air over our heads. It faded away as the bird flew off into the California skies above. The bystanders hollered in a mixture of shock and surprise. The photographer kept snapping pictures.

"It's flying away with that girl!" the Latino yelled.

"I'm calling the cops!" a gruff-voiced woman snorted. "Those Uudah people are too much! Now I have to raise the motel's rates to pay for that roof that stupid giant bird tore off."

"Hey!" the photographer called. "Can I take a picture of you? I wanna show this to my editor. He'll love this. I might even get my own byline!"

"Stow it!" The rough-voiced woman growled.

Afterwards, a long silence followed. Police car sirens broke it as they raced towards the motel. I heard their radios crackle about the big bird taking off the Happy Hideaway's roof and abducting a female victim.

"You want me to send a helicopter to pursue it?" one of the cops asked.

"Forget it!" the voice on the radio's other end moaned. "It's another one of those crazy Uudah incidents that's not worth the State's tax money. Over and out."

In the long silence that followed, I lifted my face off of the bathtub's surface. I looked at Lianne with weary eyes.

"Let's go find your boyfriend before Ian Hand sacrifices him," I said. "Turn yourself into something more comfortable, and let's go save him."

Lianne's beautiful face hardened, and her eyes narrowed at me.

"I don't have any magical powers!" She folded her arms across her chest.

Rolling my eyes towards Heaven, I said, "With God, all things are possible."

To be continued...

Two Winters
by
Lee Clark Zumpe

I shamble down the slick steps toward the sidewalk. I feel them watching me, peering through nicotine-yellowed plastic slatted blinds from windows several stories above – watching as I slip away, returning to the comfort of obscurity. For all their questioning and probing, I surrendered not one bit of information that could connect me with the crimes they believe I committed.

I knew from the beginning I would be absolved. After a few days, they had to let me go.

Dirty snow clots the gutters beneath the dingy, gray skies. It's the second day of February, and Pittsburgh has not seen the sun all year. The harsh winter has claimed its share of victims. So many fragile souls hover on the brink between life and death without custodians to watch over them: the elderly living alone in filthy, rundown tenements; the homeless curled up on park benches or pressed against trash bins in alleyways; the runaways and junkies and the deranged.

The killer knows this. He takes advantage of the weak and the unprotected.

I shuffle along side streets, down familiar avenues. Friday evening has cleared the roads, sending people to their homes or to old taverns where they will drink away the week's paycheck. They feel a little more confident today, a little less frightened. The papers published my picture prematurely; someone leaked the story. The headlines claimed the police had found the killer.

Tomorrow, they will be forced to admit their mistake. Tomorrow, the city will shudder once more.

The killer has done hideous things, things so monstrous I wept when confronted with photographs of the crime scenes. It began in November. Mutilated bodies found in the streets, screams echoing beneath the twilight. He strikes without mercy or shame. At first, the murders occurred only at night in remote areas. With time, he became bolder, more impudent. The most recent victim was found in a parked car on a busy street in the afternoon.

Darkness descends as I reach my apartment building six blocks from the police station. I suspect that I have been followed. They will not give up their only lead easily. They will not enjoy acknowledging their blunder. I do not fault them, no matter how unpleasant my incarceration was – no matter how much their accusations and brutal interrogation terrified me.

A single witness claimed to have seen me at the scene of the most recent murder. He mistook a bloodstain on my coat sleeve for the blood of the victim. The blood, I calmly told the officers the afternoon I was detained, had come from a wounded animal I had taken to the vet early in the day. Testing and inquiries validated my account.

Still, I am haunted by the images I was forced to review during my confinement. The repugnance I felt at seeing these things I cannot overemphasize. Yet, while nausea, fear, and anger overwhelmed me, I admit a certain sense of familiarity emerged. As I studied each successive picture, I felt as if I had seen the scene previously – as a detached observer, an impotent spectator compelled to watch the slaughter.

I shake the grisly thoughts as I fumble for my keys, blame the proliferation of violence on television for making commonplace those graphic images that should be both alien and repellent.

Inside, I do not bother with the lights. I am exhausted, frustrated, and shaken. In the kitchen, I run water into the sink basin where dirty dishes have sat, collecting flies in my absence. Cockroaches race beneath the refrigerator.

Moments later, I stand in front of the bathroom mirror. The man returning my gaze reminds me his work is not finished. The darkness festering in his eyes deposes me once more, sending me into exile.

I have seen my shadow and returned to my burrow. Winter will continue.

The End

Haiku III by Denny E. Marshall

Edgar Allen Poe
true cause of death the ravens
constant rap music

Dracula's Third Wife by Marge Simon

She was an ornery woman
of Spanish descent, with
an incendiary temperament,

intolerant of my excuses
for staying out past coffin-time,
suspicious of my business affairs

that took me to other countries
for negotiations imperative
to our undeadlihood.

When I arrived home just after
sunrise, she flew into a rage,
ran out of the castle shrieking

gibberish, but when the sun
rose to hit her full in the face, she
vanished in a puff of brimstone.

Oh, those days of passion!
The smell of Azahar perfume,
that lingering taste of human blood,
when all hungers were sated.

Brass Mineral Lighthouse Hospice for the Terminally Undead
by
Rajeev Bhargava

A towering Brass Mineral Lighthouse Hospice for the Terminally Undead had been built in Hell, using zombie workers, by order of the Federation of Monsters. Its presiding member was none other than Beelzebub. It stood planted in a sea of blood with its blinding beam of light. The inpatients, all monsters, of course, had been brought in by the Grim Reaper on his raft of human bones, which acted as their ambulance across the vast hot seas of blood. The reason: quite recently, a deadly pandemic had appeared and was spreading fast, infecting the monster population. This infection had no name yet, let alone a cure. Only one thing was sure. Once it was caught, it made its victims more *human,* announcing that the end was near. Only one mineral, brass, kept it at bay for a short while. The infection affected each kind of monster differently.

Inside the lighthouse, an endless row of spiral staircases led to various corridors that led to wardrooms where monster-patients were getting care. There was a secluded ward where staff provided end-of-life care under palliative care and sedation.

Inside an upper ward, a 347-year-old female ghoul stood and looked around with her blood-red eyes, drooling saliva wherever she walked.

"Would anyone fancy some nutrition?" she asked in a pained, croaky voice. She held a brass tray in her withered hands. It contained a shrunken head, smothered in a yellow intestinal pus, and a cocktail glass of blood with bat venom. She wore a PPE outfit, as all staff members did to avoid catching the infection. She gazed around at the pathetic bedridden figures. No reply or response, let alone the slightest trace of interest. As the ghoul turned to leave, one of the patients, a werewolf strapped to his bed for his own safety, roared. His eyes shifted from their normal yellow to bright red, a Stage 2 symptom of the dreaded fatal disease.

"Oh, Henreeh! I know you're in a lot of pain," the ghoul said. "Your once-yellow eyes have now turned red. Soon, it will be time to shift you downstairs. Let me have a word with Dr. Psychonster. Err … would you care for a slice of the shrunken head?"

"Rrrr!!!" Henreeh wriggled to be let free.

"Maybe later then, hmm? All right then, I'll be back again in a while.

"Oh, and do remember, everyone, to use your pain-ringers, should the need arise. Thank you all." She turned out the light, as it had just turned 9.00 p.m., then left.

No sooner had she left then one of the patients, Mrs. Gorelle, a hideous but cultured ogre on the bed opposite Henreeh, called out eloquently, "We'll all be sorry to see you go, Henreeh. You'll be sorely missed, for sure."

Over the years, she had regarded him as her pet.

Henreeh's contorted face softened, and he responded with a look which only Mrs. Gorelle recognized.

Just then, a loud creaking sound, one familiar to all the patients, announced the opening of the Hospice's main entrance door and the arrival of new patients. Their manic, cackling laughter made them sound like Hell's clowns.

From all the monsters in the Lighthouse Hospice, there were more Hell's clowns than any other. The reason for this was unclear, but according to one theory, there was an uncanny and genetic link with humans. This was just a generalized view still held by the medical team and patients alike. In fact, only *one* had managed to hold onto precious death for two years instead of one, much to the nursing team's surprise. Finally, the infection took its toll, and "Lucky," as he was nicknamed, dissolved into a red liquid goo, which evaporated into nothingness. And this was the typical manner in which all monsters in Hell were dying from the infection.

The pandemic had killed off zillions of monsters, as the medical team put their heads together in a desperate bid to develop a vaccine to save them.

Meanwhile, in a private medical room, a consultant mummy paced up and down the room with one of his witch assistants, holding a pipette in both hands, nervously facing a beaker on the laboratory desk.

"All right, Cursella, now very carefully drop some of the serum into the beaker. We don't want any more accidents, do we?" he said with contempt in his fiery green eyes.

"Of course not, Dr. Tep. I'm sorry about the incident earlier today."

With the greatest of care, she poured some of the serum, but the pipette smashed in her withered but powerful grip.

"Curses!" cried Dr. Tep, infuriated. He extended his right bandaged arm towards the door. "Get out. *Now*!"

"I'm sorry, Dr. Tep; really, I am. You … you're making me nervous."

"Leave! Or else I shall have to call the Orc security guards to throw you into the river of blood."

As Cursella left, slamming the door, the doctor shrugged and placed his decayed hands over his bandaged face.

"Holy Isis, the kind of monsters I have to put up with! I shall *have* to complain to Satan about her, for sure."

Outside, as if in response, the thunder roared. Hailstones belted down from the dark, eerie skies, where gargoyles were in flight, high above the eerie-looking lighthouse.

There was a loud thud, like a falling sound, followed by concerned voices. It was coming from a ward two flights of stairs above. At that moment, Cursella was midway up the stairs, sobbing, then went rushing to the room in time to see a yellow goo dripping from the bed onto the floor. One of the patients, known as Alfred-B, had just disintegrated then dissolved into nothingness. Even the goo disappeared, as was usually the case, so there was never any need to clean up. Cursella looked around wide-eyed at the inpatients, all of which were Hell's skeletons, and asked,

"Did any of you see what happened to Alf before he disintegrated?"

"I did." replied the inpatient directly facing her, from the opposite bed. "Just before his last moment, he called out, almost in a human voice."

"What did he say?"

"He cried, 'help!' then began to change; liquidate into yellow puss … and…"

"Go on," Cursella prodded.

"I saw the glimpse of a human face just before he disintegrated," the inpatient told her.

Cursella sighed, then looked around.

"I'm so sorry you all had to witness this. Now try and rest your tired bones." She turned out the lights, then left.

****

The following Morning, Dr. Tep entered the same ward with a medical briefcase. His dishevelled face cracked into a smile, causing some of the decay on his mummified skin to fall through the bandages and onto the floor.

"Good news to share, dear inpatients. I think we may have an antidote for the infection. But first, a little briefing. We think we may know how the disease came about. He looked around at the skeletons who sat up attentively on their beds.

"Gargoyles!" he said in a triumphant voice. "Yes, because only *they* are the ones who have not been affected. We believe that they are spreading it everywhere."

"But gargoyles have been flying around for centuries in Hell," one of the skeletons said. "Why now?"

Dr. Tep shrugged. "Like us, gargoyles have their own biological anatomy. The infection may have derived from them," he repeated with emphasis.

"That's silly," called out Darkelisa-Z, a female skeleton. Each of the skeletons had an alphabetical number tag against their names to identify them. "How can you possibly deduce this?"

"Look around you," Dr. Tep said. "Each and every monster on our planet is infected, *except* the gargoyles."

"I wonder what Beelzebub has to say about that," Michaellus-R folded his arms in his bed.

"In any case, I have developed an antidote and need to try it out on a few volunteers." Dr. Tep looked around. "Who would like to go first?"

Once again, there was a loud noise, but this time, it was no thud. It was a pained scream that quieted a few seconds, then a short silence and hissing. Dr. Tep's eyes widened. He dropped the large syringe in his left hand, causing the serum to sizzle and dissolve on the floor. He left the ward abruptly and went down to his room, got out a shielding PPE mirror helmet, then continued to the basement to the Medusa Ward.

Once there, he kicked down the door with his mummified right leg and stormed inside. There before him, on the floor, immersed in a pool of blood sat the three daughters of Echidna and Typhon, namely ~ Stheno, Euryale, and the hideous, ugly Medusa with her head of snakes. Her head was soaked in red blood.

"What do you want in here? Hsss!!" called out a threatening monotonous voice from behind the door that had struck him. Dr. Tep moved back and saw the fourth gorgon. This one was male, and he was their guardian. His name was Nanas, the guard of Zeus. They were among the oldest inpatients of Beelzebub's Lighthouse Hospice and the scariest and deadliest. No monster came near them, lest they turn to stone.

"I heard a loud cry. What happened in here?" asked Dr. Tep.

"We're having our lunch!" Stheno cried in a shrill voice.

"You've committed a murder. I will report you to Dr. Psychonster!"

"It is merely a gargoyle that smashed through our ward window. Look." She pointed to a smashed window on the far end of the room.

Dr. Tep raised an eyebrow.

"I have to warn you that in my research, I have found that the infection may derive from gargoyles. But I have devised a serum and would like to try it on all of you, to save your miserable undead lives, of course.

"Now, if you refuse, you will die a horrible death. The flesh of that wretched gargoyle may be infected."

The gorgons looked at one another, hissing. They broke into a fight. Dr. Tep gave a sadistic laugh, then left. He locked the door on the way out and made his way back to his private room. At the same moment, outside, the Grim Reaper brought in his latest patient, a hideous scarred demon. The hospice doors creaked open, and the Reaper pointed a bony finger, ushering him to make his way up the stairs. Then he glided out, slamming the door shut. The demon made his way upstairs, and some of the staff, all ogres, appeared and aided him up.

"Oh, we don't often get demons in here," an ogre said. "What's your name?"

He stared back at her and replied in a slow, pained voice due to a slash on his neck, "Jack."

She engraved his name on a brass band and placed it around his left arm.

The ground beneath their feet shook, and Beelzebub's voice echoed around the cold walls.

"Stop! This monstrosity is so evil and capable of unnamed horrors that he does not deserve *any* form of care in our hospice, let alone a place in Hell. There is only one punishment for him: he will be exiled to Earth and be remembered for his evil deeds, as the most infamous killer of all … Jack the Ripper! Moreover, his real identity will remain unknown forever."

In a few seconds, Jack vanished and was gone…

The End

Shadows by Josh Maybrook

Throughout my brief existence, I have been
Beleaguered by a force that renders all
The happiness in life a dismal pall.
This force is to the human eye unseen
Yet manifest in shadows tall and lean
That weirdly twist and writhe and crawl
And dance nightmarishly on every wall
Like grim projections cast upon a screen.
No future solace lies in store for me;
No hope is there of one day being shown
Some mercy from the gods who've destined me
To face these shadow-menaces alone.
For, all too well, I know I cannot flee:
The shadows that oppress me are my own.

Raw Liver
by
Marge Simon

My Unknown One, where are you now? I search my waking self to no avail—you have been so close with me for weeks—it is as if you have vanished. I hear rustling in corners of my room. I'm afraid to look.

Such dreams I've had! Terrible, terrible dreams. I fear to sleep. The skies are overcast and dull, by day. Many nights I cannot see the moon, nor yet a single star. Our lovely garden is starkly barren, save for nocturnal creatures. If I'm up to sitting on a cold stone bench long enough, I can see their beady eyes glowing under the bushes. It is a different place, alive and not.

Mama persists in enticing me to eat. It's so hard for me to get even a morsel of meat into my mouth. But if it's not well done, I manage a few bites. Mama noticed this and tonight, I was served a plate of raw liver. The smell was repugnant. I wouldn't touch the frightful thing—its color similar to Father Martin's mottled face when he starts bloviating about sin. Yet strangely, when I soaked up the bloodied juices with one of cook's fresh rolls, I found it rather to my liking. Mama was pleased.

The End

*From Mina's role in **The Demeter Diaries**, Marge Simon (Mina) Bryan Dietrich (Vlad), Independent Legions, 2019, Winner of the Lord Ruthven Assembly Award for Best Fiction Novel, Bram Stoker Finalist*

Sleeping Beauty by Matthew Wilson

Today I have kissed a queen
into the museum I did dare
to the casket of the creature
with dead serpents in her hair.

I never welshed on a bet
now the world will know
that I am the bravest fool
to kiss her lips as white as snow.

The dead queen was a tyrant
burning men of histories' pages
before she was betrayed and killed
to save her hate from all the ages.

Now I have dared to this museum
to kiss the queen that all despise
when I had thought myself so brave
until she opened those hateful eyes.

Sleepless Nights
by
Marge Simon

O love, these nights I find it increasingly impossible to sleep. Mama worries so. She says I've grown thin as wheat and summons Doctor Seward. He prescribes an opiate. The pills are small, easy to tuck them under my tongue and pretend to swallow. Sarah brings me hot chocolate and tea cakes fresh from Cook's oven, yet I've no appetite. How I wish they'd stop fussing over me. Only a few days, and they are so concerned! It's not food that I crave—I am consumed with passion for a man I've never met. I'd so like to confide these feelings with my dear friend Miss Lucy, but she is terribly unwell these days. Besides, it would never do for me to be unfaithful to Jonathan. I should feel such shame—and of course I would, if these recent fantasies were real. And yet, here I am telling *you* my feelings!

Tonight, I have Sarah draw my bath and dismiss her. I soak the sponge and let it linger in certain places as I wash. I imagine your hands caressing my skin, your lips between my thighs—I blush to think of such a thing! But it is true, I would deny you nothing. The bath salts turn the water the color of sweet grapes. I find this quite pleasing, for it matches the veins in my arms. The scent is hypnotic. I don't try to understand what this means, but it seems as if you are so close.

When I open the tallest windows in my room, the air is warm and moist, breathing on its own. I bite my lips into a shade you'd like, wipe away the drops.

The End

*From Mina's role in **The Demeter Diaries**, Marge Simon (Mina) Bryan Dietrich (Vlad), Independent Legions, 2019, Winner of the Lord Ruthven Assembly Award for Best Fiction Novel, Bram Stoker Finalist*

Simon Wallow
by
Christopher Dabrowski

They went to the Late Cretaceous period to get samples of plants and bring the most interesting species back to life. The crew of Aurora Time Drome included: Captain Simon Wallow; his brother, Franz Willow; his daughter, Res Wallow; and an Archibald von den Knorr, a non-family member.

Everything was as per the plan; it was a standard expedition. Using crosslinked laser beams, they bent gravity, creating the so-called gravity funnel, which also serves as a time-space tunnel. And they flew to the period when dinosaurs ruled the Earth. They collected the required samples and set off to get back to their time.

Simon Willow woke from a nightmare covered in sweat. His heart pounded like a furious death metal drummer. His mouth was as dry as during Holo-history lectures, where he had a hangover simulator experience.

Of course, to better understand alcohol intoxication and why people put themselves through such suffering, he tried the intoxication simulator. Then, he understood his great-grand-ancestors.

He dreamed that he woke up in ancient times when people were ugly. The walls of the room were covered with something peeling off them. The thing was called *wallpaper*.

He was lying on a terribly uncomfortable lounger called a *bed*.

The poor people must have been unhappy, he thought, knowing that it was still two centuries before a molecular cloud adjusting to the body would be invented. Next to him, there was his wife, but she didn't look like herself. She was fat... but everybody knew that nano-fat-burners eliminated the disease a long time before. And she was making scary sounds!

His sound identifier scanned the database and provided the thought-answer that was decoded by Captain Wallow's brain within a fraction of a second. It was the so-called *snoring*, a condition that was quite frequent at those times.

Luckily, he was just dreaming. He looked around his room and yawned with relief.

Archibald stood at the sleeping cabin sluice. "Captain, my captain," Knorr mumbled, pale as Snow White. "Frank's having his attack!"

Simon gulped. "An attack? Now? That's strange..."

He rose to his feet from his delightedly soft molecular cloud.

And by the way, how could he have a nightmare? *Oh, right … I forgot the sleep regulators,* he chided himself, because it was his fault that they took too few capsules. Being a responsible captain, when he realized that he had overlooked this detail, he divided his dose between the rest of the crew. He thus forfeited the pleasant dreams guaranteed by the product manufacturer.

He sent a mental command to a solid layer of intelligent molecules surrounding his body to change from pajamas to a captain's uniform. The holowear had many other advantages, too; it could generate a soft sensation under his feet, which allowed him to move without a single sound. Upon leaving the living premises, it changed into a holosuit adjusting to external conditions. In winter, it provided heat; in summer, it cooled. It also maintained the skin and cleaned the body from sweat, sebum, and other organic debris.

If necessary, one could even become invisible.

Captain Wallow and Knorr hurried to the main chamber, passing four sluices that dematerialized themselves when the walking persons were identified as authorized to enter.

What they found, when they arrived, was ghastly.

Res Wallow, with quite a unique name—her mother, Un Swallow, loved original, yet old-fashioned names—was standing, pale, in front of a mental pit, not knowing what to do. She was observing Franz Willow, who wriggled around the room with his eye whites running to the back of his skull and shouting sequences of words:

"Herd. Partner. Change. New. Swallow. Nine on ten. Promotion. Hierarchy. Eggs! Eggs! Eggs!"

Franz had natural medium abilities. When they were getting close to their destination, i.e., a defining year in ancient times, he would enter a hypnotic state and let himself get possessed by the *ghost of times,* as people used to call the gathered consciousness created by the whole humanity.

Franz was always acquiring this state purposely, but now...

"He... he... we were just talking, and he got like this." Res Wallow was trying to explain, but she couldn't find the right words. Meanwhile, Franz started hopping around the room, waving his hands as if he were a bird and swinging like a swallow. "Squawk! Squawk! Squawk!"

Res, amazed, sat down and bit her nails, staring without paying any attention to the anti-biter that was beeping louder and louder.

Gulp! The swallowing attack wasn't over.

Oh, I could sure use some black coffee for this swallowing of mine. Captain Wallow sighed. But he knew that he must get himself together after his recent nightmare and bravely face the current, real terror.

"Something demented him," Knorr growled.

"Something possessed him, I believe," Simon corrected him.

Everything was clicking into the right place in his head, making a logical whole. Squawking from the possessed Franz. And that series of words...

One moment, what was that?

Gulp!

"I've got it!" He remembered what he knew about swallows. Their flocks had a strict hierarchy. The male alpha, the leader of the flock, is number one. He mates with a female, also number one, the most attractive in the flock. And if the flock has seven males and seven females, then the weakest male mates with the female number seven. If male six were to die, get disabled in any way, and lose his position in the ranking, then male seven would take his place and mate with his female, number six.

Yes, all the words shouted by Franz fit the swallows perfectly. All apart from one...

What about the eggs? And why was his brother's mind possessed by the spirits of birds when they were returning to their time?

Even when he sipped his black coffee and ate chocolate kisses, the question remained unanswered. For goodness sake, the answers would always come to his mind when he sipped coffee and ate the fucking kisses. But this time none - total emptiness!

The answer came just as they landed in the target year. Franz, who couldn't be awoken from the possession, had to be gagged, tied, and laid on a cloud in his cabin.

After that, they all went to the airlock. Vapor puffed, something hissed and cracked, just like it used to do in ancient times in science fiction films – and the airlock opened. They saw something that amazed them.

Hundreds, thousands, or maybe even several thousands of eggs. Swallow eggs. These were much larger as if the swallow that laid the eggs was larger than an ostrich! Apart from this anomaly, these were typical swallow eggs. The shells were off-white, with dark reddish or brownish spots.

"This is crazy!" Knorr growled.

"Uh-oh!" Res's voice cracked.

They were in an enormous modern hall, with high temperatures, so the holozones automatically switched to cooling. After a few steps, they were standing on the floor, and then they appeared—no one knew where from. From all directions, giant swallows dressed in military uniforms were running towards them.

Their wings had attachments looking like blasters of something. Simon was not interested in checking exactly was blasting out of them.

"Retreat," he ordered quietly but firmly. "To the airlock, we'll be safe there."

And despite the giant, mutated swallows running towards them, step by step, cold-blooded, Simon and his crew retreated to the airlock. The swallows were running on muscular limbs that would be better suited for dinosaurs, squawking louder and louder.

However, the tactic was effective. Simon and his crew retreated slowly, without making any of the aggressors use his or her gun. Yet, they didn't know the firing range of these guns. When they reached the force field of the time drome, the swallows aimed their weapons at the team, squawking more and more impatiently.

Well, it looks like we are the aggressors here, Simon thought. *This sure doesn't look like Earth.*

Series fired from the birds' blasters splashed against the invisible protection field and flowed down to the ground. The liquid must have been acid since it corroded the tiles with a loud hiss. Squeaking, cracking, and throwing vapor, the airlock door finally closed, shutting them away from the unfriendly world.

"This is my fault, my fault!" Res Wallow was crying in despair.

"How come?" Knorr asked.

Simon froze in midstep. He guessed what he would hear from his daughter. Res broke the most important rule: not to take any living things into the past, apart from humans.

Of course, Res did it, thinking that nothing bad would happen if she took her beloved swallows for a ride. They were so lovely, so good, and so intelligent. Well, that was the clue—*intelligent*!

Genetic modifications made Percival and Amber—that were the swallows' names—were "tuned up" to such a degree that they knew almost 300 words and could construct simple sentences. They could add and subtract, although with some difficulty. And Res took those mutated birds to the times when dinosaurs ruled the Earth. The swallows were intelligent enough to escape when they found the right moment.

Res kept them in an old-fashioned cage without any electronic protection. But such an intelligent bird can open the lock after practicing some lockpicking. And what happened? Mother Nature, along with Auntie Evolution, did their thing. So, this is still Earth ... but not our Earth! And humankind?

Most probably, humankind didn't even have the chance to exist. It was pecked away by intelligent swallows.

Simon collapsed.

The End

Why Is?
by
Kevin R. Doyle

"Grandma, why is the sky blue?"

The little girl stands out on the enclosed patio, looking at the outside world through the once clear, but now nearly opaque, plexiglass. She's wearing a light blue dress and white tennis shoes, the same outfit as always, and with her back to me, I admire her short, blonde curls.

They almost look lifelike.

"Why, Grandma?" she says without turning to look at me. "Why is the sky blue?"

I cudgel my brain, trying to remember the answer from school nearly sixty years before, all while knowing she doesn't really expect an answer. This has been happening a lot lately, the seemingly random questions coming from what appears to be a four-year-old girl.

Whoever constructed her no doubt intended it to be merely another trait to add verisimilitude to the conceit, but I really wish they hadn't bothered.

After all, four-year-old questions quickly become tiresome.

****

She's (notice I don't address her by name, seeing as I have no clue where she came from, let alone her name) spending more and more time out on the enclosed patio these days, while I barely stir from my old rocking chair, all the way across the living room, which has two large doors that open out onto the patio.

In the more normal past, those doors usually stayed shut. With the shoreline only a hundred yards away, all manner of dirt and critters could have invaded the house. But then, as the news got progressively worse, and the lockdowns and quarantines which began in Europe started marching across the globe, Roger went to the trouble and expense of installing the large, transparent plexiglass shell that completely encloses the patio. We got into the habit of throwing open the doors, which gave the illusion of a wide-open space throughout the house.

Minus the invasion of critters.

It seemed a good idea at the time, and Roger installed the material even before the majority of government mandates on how best to combat the scourge. But we didn't realize that things would stay so permanent, and shortly before he passed away, Roger grumbled at the fact that the once-clear barrier had begun to dull and darken.

Even when I stand right up against it, as I occasionally still do, my old eyes can't see much besides murk. But if I listen as hard as I can, and there's no other sound, I can sometimes hear the surf crashing against the shore.

I haven't actually seen that shore in I'm not sure how long. By now, it's pretty clear I never will again, no matter how long I live.

Which, all things considered, won't be long now.

"Grandma," the little one, now standing in the doorway to my bedroom, says, "why is grass green?"

I can almost answer that one, the solution on the tip of my tongue, but I'm too tired now to talk. And why start now?

I've only once spoken to the little girl that inhabits my house with me.

****

It wasn't the COVID-19, that unexpected disaster of the early twenty-first century that did us in. The world recovered from that, more or less, in a relatively brief blip of time.

However, twenty years later, COVID-19's bigger, nastier, more rapid cousin came along. Before you knew it, the lockdowns and quarantines of 2020 were like a game of hide and seek compared to what happened. The disease this time was unrelenting.

A mortality rate of one or two percent, which had seemed so apocalyptic a few decades before?

Hah.

Try forty, fifty, in some countries, sixty percent, at least that they reported, and you'd begin to envision what we experienced. It wasn't a return to 2020, more like a return to the 14th Century, with the plague running rampant across the world.

Roger and I were lucky that we had the means to take care of ourselves, including his plexiglass installation along the back patio. In the early days of the quarantine, we would sometimes get out in the morning, the sun barely up, and walk along the beach, hand in hand, just as we had in the first years of our marriage.

Before too long, though, dead and rotting bodies, mainly of the homeless, began to infest the beach, as if they'd come to experience one nice spot before they passed away, so we ended our morning sojourns.

The news became spotty at best, mainly just a robotic recitation of mortality figures, peppered with brief reports of government efforts to quell the disease. Eventually, we stopped listening to all that.

One by one, our friends and family ceased to communicate with us online, leading us to assume that they'd taken ill as well.

If there was any report of a guardian program being instituted, we missed it, so it was quite a shock to wake up one morning, stumble from our bedroom and see the little blonde girl in her blue dress sitting at the table, waiting for a breakfast that we soon discovered she couldn't eat.

"Hi, Grandma and Grandpa," she called out cheerily, and I remember Roger and I both clutched each other's arms, fearful we would fall over from shock.

****

Now she's back out on the patio, rummaging around by my potting materials. As I watch her, she seems to waver in and out around the edges, as if the reception's a little off.

On the other hand, that could just be my eyes getting even worse as the days wear on.

"Grandma," she says, her back to me, almost talking in rote, "when dogs die, do they go to Heaven?"

****

Roger caught it first. Despite all our precautions, somehow or other, it came to him. Maybe on a wisp of air, passing over the beach of rotting corpses, then searching till it found a microscopic crack in our walls. Regardless of how it happened, one day, upon waking up, Roger found he couldn't quite make it out of bed, his muscles spent and helpless in his body.

The little girl somehow sent and implanted into our house by someone, most likely the government, stood by and did nothing. From her first appearance, it didn't take us long to realize she wasn't alive, not even physical in the normal sense. Composed merely of light rays and some sort of computer intelligence, she was a projection more than anything else.

With what little was left to the Internet, we'd attempted to research to find out where she came from and how she'd gotten to us. We found no records, nothing in America or anywhere else, leaving us to deduce that the authorities had somehow constructed and sent this projection to keep us company.

Decades before, after the COVID-19 scare had more or less, but not entirely gone away, the social scientists and psychologists had begun their investigations. Among other things, it was determined that the initial quarantining at the onset of that pandemic had led to sharply increased rates of dementia, apprehension, and premature death, especially among the elderly.

So the most Roger and I could determine because no matter how much we questioned the girl, she remained puzzled as to what we wanted, was that some sort of brainstorming session had led to planting these quasi-humans in the homes of elderly people, to provide comfort and consolation as the weeks and months of this new, even more terrible, pandemic marched on.

It wasn't much of a theory, and even ordinary folks like us could see all sorts of holes in it, but it was the most we could think of.

Then, of course, we didn't have much time to think at all once Roger became sick.

One good thing about this illness, whatever it is. It doesn't take long to cycle through. By the evening of his first day, Roger was tasting blood in his mouth. By the second night, he'd passed on, his body bloated in his favorite chair, dried blood trailing from mouth, nose, and ears.

I'm too old and far too weak, not to mention being hobbled by my arthritis, to do anything about getting rid of his body. But assuming that the projection of the little girl came from someone in authority gave me an idea. I pointed Roger out to her, told her he'd died, then went to bed.

In bed that night, despite the fact it was summertime, I felt colder and lonelier than ever in my life. It had been a long time since I'd slept alone, and feeling the emptiness beside me kept me up all night.

The next morning, after I'd managed to rouse myself from a faint slumber and headed out to the main room, I saw Roger's body was gone.

Wildly, I glanced around the house. No signs of anyone coming or going, no trace that anyone had been there, and my little companion sitting on the kitchen floor staring at the wall.

For sure, then. Someone, somewhere, was keeping as much of a handle on things as they could.

The only problem being, their planning was off in places. For some reason, they made my little companion a bit too much like a four-year-old. The incessant questions I didn't know the answers to, while they remind me a lot of my own grandchildren (quite possibly long dead now), tend to grate on my brain.

Not much of a problem now, though, as this morning, the aches in my muscles, more obvious than the usual ones associated with age, began. I felt a little blood trickling out of my right ear.

****

"Grandma?" Her voice has a slightly more plaintive note than before. Or maybe my hearing is simply going. I somehow made it out to my rocking chair this morning, got myself swaddled in a big, blue blanket. I intend to sit here and rock until the sickness takes me, which at my age should only be in another day or so.

"Grandma?" she repeats, definitely blurry now, but I'm positive it's my failing vision and not any defect in her programming. "Are you feeling sick?"

I hesitate to answer. If I say yes, will whoever sent her come and take me away before my time? She didn't seem to notice Roger's death until I pointed it out, but how can I know exactly how these things work?

I don't want to be taken away yet. I want to die in my own home, right here where Roger passed on. So I'll just keep quiet, not answer her, and maybe she'll get the message and leave me alone.

I had a dream last night, one of a handful in the last few years that I remember well, and it had to do with all the homes in the country and all the apartments and houses around the world. Is there a similar projection in everyone? Maybe not a little girl, but something taking the form of a cousin? A grown-up protector?

Maybe even a family pet?

If so, what will happen when the last actual person passes on? Will the world become merely a collection of empty former homes, each with a little boy or girl ceaselessly asking questions? Waiting for answers that will never come?

Is that how the race ends? With little children everywhere, in unison, asking empty rooms, "Why is the sky blue?"

****

Not much longer, now. For the last day or so, I've been coughing up blood almost continuously. An assortment of hand towels scattered around my chair is thick with the dried evidence of my illness. Everything is growing dim, much dimmer even than the view out of the opaque patio shield. At this moment, I want nothing more than one last walk along the beach with Roger.

Maybe tomorrow.

I haven't heard or seen her for hours now. Either I simply can't see or hear much, or she's gone away somewhere. Maybe back to whoever sent her.

Then, a flicker out of the corner of my eye. Glancing to the side (how painful even such a simple motion as turning the head) and she's there, but with an expression on her face, I'd never seen before.

No longer that blank, unwavering gaze. Now, somehow, she appears concerned, her features drawn into a semblance of approaching sorrow.

Is it possible, somehow, that they programmed this projection to actually feel?

"Grandma," she said, her voice barely above a whisper, "what does death feel like?"

I wonder if she means of an individual person or an entire race.

This question of hers, at least, I'll soon know the answer to.

The End

Poisoned Blood by Matthew Wilson

Shadows never settle in this house
This old tomb of my ancestors
Rocked to ruin by the nearby sea
Threatening to fall down seagull-engulfed cliffs.

Time should not have spared these stones
Resting places of maniacs and haters of men
Who still smile in my reflection
Whose memories live on in my awful dreams.

How many times have I washed my hands in that sea?
Like lady Macbeth after some great treason?
Quivering at the town posters of missing men
Whose faces haunt my midnight still.

I should not have come back to this evil place
These ruins of my ancestors are not for the living
Still scarred with the cleansing flame of heroes
Who tried to rid the world of Tepes.

About the Contributors

Linda Barrett:
Ms. Barrett has been writing all her life. She wrote her first book at the age of eight. It's still in the McKinley Elementary school library. She was published in the *Huntingdon Junior Library* literary magazine by age thirteen. She's won three awards with the Montgomery County Community College Writer's contest. "Mr. Cat's Revenge" won third place in the 2014 MCCC contest. Ms. Barrett lives with her 84 years young mother in Abington in the same house for 50 years."

Rajeev Bhargava:
Rajeev lives in Harrow with his parents and five Chihuahuas. He has been writing since the age of twelve but had his first work published in 1990. Since then he's been writing stories, poems and articles for the small press as well as mainstream. His ambition is to be a freelance writer.

Keily Blair:
Keily Blair is a creative writing student at UT Chattanooga. Her fiction has appeared in Nth Degree. She is currently at work on a fantasy novel and a collection of essays about being a person with bipolar disorder.

Margaret L. Carter:
Reading *Dracula* at the age of twelve ignited Margaret L. Carter's interest in a wide range of speculative fiction and inspired her to become a writer. Vampires, however, have always remained close to her heart. Her work on vampirism in literature includes *Dracula: The Vampire and the Critics*, *The Vampire in Literature*, *A Critical Bibliography*, and *Different Blood: The Vampire as Alien*. She holds a PhD in English from the University of California (Irvine), and her dissertation contained a chapter on *Dracula*. In fiction, she has written horror, fantasy, and paranormal romance. Recent publications include *Crimson Dreams* (vampire romance), *Demon's Fall* (paranormal romance novella), *Heart's Desires and Dark Embraces* (story collection, fantasy and paranormal romance), and *Legacy of Magic* (sword and sorcery, in collaboration with her husband, Leslie Roy Carter). Her short stories have been published in anthologies such as the "Sword and Sorceress" and "Darkover" volumes, among others. "A Walk in the Mountains," co-written with her husband, appeared in the 2016 anthology *Realms of Darkover*. A sequel, "Believing," was included in *Masques of Darkover* (2017). Margaret's solo humorous ghost story, "Haunted Book Nook," appeared in the anthology *Sword and Sorceress* 33 (2018). She and her husband, a retired naval officer, live in Maryland and have four sons, several grandchildren and great-grandchildren, a St. Bernard, and two cats.

Christopher T. Dabrowski:
Christopher has had numerous books published in the USA and Poland. His USA works include: *Anomaly* and *Escape*, both published by the Royal Hawaiian Press. Books published in Poland include *Anima Vilis* (Initium), *Grobbing* (Novae Res), *Deathbirth and other Stories* (Agharta & Amoryka), *Orgazmokalipsa* (Alternatywne publishing house), *Anomalia* (Forma publishing house), and *Ucieczka* (2017 - Dom Horroru publishing house). Monika Olasek provided the English translation for his *Night to Dawn* stories.

Sandy DeLuca:
Sandy has written five novels; *Settling in Nazareth* (she painted the cover art), *Descent*, *Manhattan Grimoire*, *From Ashes*, and *Requiem for the Dead*. Her poetry chapbook, *Burial Plot in Sagittarius* (also created cover art and illustrations), was nominated for the BRAM STOKER award in 2001. Her art has been exhibited in galleries, hair salons, book stores and online venues. She has also painted covers and contributed interior illustrations for various numerous small press venues.

Kevin R. Doyle:
A high-school teacher, former college instructor and fiction writer, Kevin R. Doyle is the author of three crime thrillers, *The Group*, *When You Have to Go There*, and *And the Devil Walks Away*, published by MuseItUp

Publications, and one horror novel, *The Litter*, published by Night to Dawn Magazine and Books. This year also saw the release of the first book in his Sam Quinton mystery series, *Squatter's Rights*, by Camel Press. Next year should see the release of the second Sam Quinton novel, *Heel Turn*. Doyle teaches English and speech at a high school in central Missouri.

Chris Friend:

Chris has published his art in small press horror magazines for nearly 25 years. His surreal horror images have been featured in *Stygian Articles, Realm of the Vampire, Deathrealm, Black Petals,* and *Space and Time*. He draws his inspiration from Harry Clarke, H. R. Giger, and the horror comics of the 70s such as the Tomb of Dracula her and the Hammer Studios Frankenstein films. Chris friend can be reached at Mars_art_13@yahoo.com. Chris friend can be reached at Mars_art_13@yahoo.com.

To sample his illustrations, go to http://chris.michaelherring.net and http://www.moonlit-path.com/art-2-13-06.htm.

Todd Hanks:

The creative writing of Todd Hanks has been seen in publications such as Asimov's Science Fiction Magazine and the Kansas City Star newspaper.

Samuel Junior Irusota:

Samuel Junior Irusota is a multiple award-winning Nigerian poet, author, and lawyer. He is the author of *A Boy's Body Is War*. He is also the author of two chapbooks entitled *The Day God Died* and *Innocent Murderers*. He won the Wakaso Poetry Contest in March, 2020. He won the Clash of Pens Poetry Contest in 2019. He was a joint Winner of the Poets in Nigeria Food Poetry Contest in 2018. He was shortlisted for the Eriata Oribhabor Poetry Prize in 2019 and the ZI Prize for Literature in 2019. He was Shortlisted for the Poetically Written Prose Contest in 2018 and the Nigerian students Poetry Prize in 2018. His works have appeared in *Trouvaille Review, Merak* magazine, *Journal Nine, Tush* magazine, *Praxis* magazine, *Inverse Journal, Indian Periodical,* and elsewhere. He believes that poetry is a tool with which we can change the world. He writes from Edo State in Nigeria.

Hal Kempka:

Hal's stories have been published in numerous magazines and ezines including *Night to Dawn, Blood Moon Rising, Black Petals, Inner Sins, Sanitarium, Yellow Mama,* and *Microhorror*. His horror short fiction anthologies, *Blue Plate Special* and *Discarded Treasures,* are currently available on Amazon Kindle, Barnes and Noble, and Smashwords, among others. *Discarded Treasures* is available in both paperback and e-book. Other anthologies including his stories are Pill Hill Press: *Zombie Art Inspired Short Stories, Blood Bound Books: Seasons in the Abyss,* and Post Mortem Press: *Shadowplay.*

Tom Johnson:

Tom, a Vietnam veteran with twenty years in the military police (L.E.), has enjoyed literary success as a science fiction novelist with his action adventures in the Jurassic Period of Earth's predawn. He has created short story SF characters like Captain Danger of the *Space Rangers* and the galactic master thief, *The Forever Man* as futuristic space opera adventure. His many costumed crime fighters include two of his own creations, such as *The Black Ghost* and *The Masked Avenger,* as well as a western masked hero of the plains called *The Nightwind*. He has upcoming stories of *Ki-Gor the Jungle Lord,* and Greek heroes like Hercules and Atalanta. For the latest information on Tom and his writing, check out his websites:

http://www15.brinkster.com/jur1/index.html
www.geocities.com/fadingshadows1/index.html.

Rod Marsden:

Rod Marsden hails from Sydney, Australia. He has three degrees related to writing and history. His stories have been published in Australia, England, Russia, the USA and now Canada. He has work in the American anthology *Cats Do it Better,* the American steam punkanthology *Break Time* and in the Canadian anthology *Morbid Metamorphosis*. Many of his short stories have been published in *Night to Dawn* magazine. His books include *Undead Reb Down Under and Other Vampire Stories, Disco Evil: Dead Man's Stand, Ghost Dance,* and *Desk Job* (his salute to Lewis Carroll). *Cold Water Conscience* is his venture into Crime/Horror. His short play, *Zombie*

Vision, was well received at Cronulla Arts Theatre. His play *Hyde and Seek* was even better received. Rod has a fondness for Cronulla and the Wollongong area but an abiding love for the more northern Clarence River region of his home state of New South Wales.

Denny E. Marshall:

Denny E. Marshall has had art, poetry, and fiction published. Some recent credits include interior art in *Midnight Echo #14* Dec. 2019, cover art for *Society Of Misfit Stories* Feb. 2020, and poetry in *Space & Time Magazine #134* Fall 2019. This year his website is celebrating 20 years on the web. Also in 2020 his artwork is for sale for the first time. It is available on Zazzle as posters coffee cups, puzzles, mouse pads, etc. The link is on his website. (Click on top left drawing.) See more at www.dennymarshall.com.

James Masters:

James was born in Tampa, Florida. When he was 16, his father died in an auto accident. This led to him moving to Ohio, and eventually, Parkersburg, West Virginia. He now works in Security and illustrates fantasy. He's been sketching since an early age and plans to send more illustrations to be featured in Night to Dawn.

Josh Maybrook:

Josh Maybrook is a writer of horror and dark fantasy based in Philadelphia, Pennsylvania. He enjoys book collecting and counts Arthur Machen, H.P. Lovecraft, and Robert Aickman among his favorite authors. Recent appearances include poems in *Spectral Realms* and *Lovecraftiana*.

Elizabeth Hattie Pierce-Collins:

Elizabeth first learned art and drawing from her mother. From there, she was self-taught until she was able to attend art school. She loves drawing the human figure and never stops studying the human body in motion. Her illustrations have appeared in *Night to Dawn* magazine and *The Spider's Web* (a novel). These have drawn positive attention from the readers. Elizabeth hopes to appear in more magazines and books in the future. For more information, contact Elizabeth at wackyursalinan45@aol.com.

Baishampayan Seal:

Baishampayan Seal is based in Kolkata, India, where they are currently pursuing an MSc in Statistics. When not testing hypotheses or beating the keyboard for C++ or R coding, they spend time weaving short poems and flash stories. Their work has previously appeared or is forthcoming in *Bewildering Stories* (http://www.bewilderingstories.com/issue859/questions_stay.html), *Utopia Science Fiction* (https://www.utopiasciencefiction.com/product-page/august-2020-vol-2-issue-01), *Scifaikuest* and *Star*Line* (https://www.sfpoetry.com/sl/issues/starline43.3.html), among others. Find them on twitter @BaishampayanSe1.

Marge Simon:

Marge Simon's works appear in publications such as DailySF Magazine, Pedestal, Dreams& Nightmares. She edits a column for the HWA Newsletter, "Blood & Spades: Poets of the Dark Side," and serves as Chair of the Board of Trustees. She won the Strange Horizons Readers Choice Award, 2010, and the SFPA's Dwarf Stars Award, 2012. She has won three Bram Stoker Awards ® for Superior Work in Poetry, two first place Rhysling Awards and the Grand Master Award from the SF Poetry Association, 2015. In addition to her poetry, she has published two prose collections: *Christina's World*, Sam's Dot Publications, 2008 and *Like Birds in the Rain*, Sam's Dot, 2007. Her poems appear in *Qualia Nous* (Written Backwards), *The Dark Phantastique* (Jasunni Productions), Spectral Realms anthologies by S.T. Joshi, and more poems will appear in *Chiral Mad 3* and *Scary Out There*, a HWA/ Simon & Schuster Y/A collection, 2015. www.margesimon.com

Matthew Wilson:

Matthew Wilson has had over 150 appearances in such places as *Horror Zine, Star*Line, Spellbound, Illumen, Apokrupha Press, Gaslight Press, Sorcerers Signal* and many more. He is currently editing his first novel and can be contacted on twitter @matthew94544267.

Lee Clark Zumpe:

Lee Clark Zumpe has been writing and publishing horror, dark fantasy and speculative fiction since the late 1990s. His short stories and poetry have appeared in a variety of publications such as *Weird Tales, Space and Time* and *Dark Wisdom;* and in anthologies such as *Dark Horizons, Best New Zombie Tales Vol. 3, Dread Shadows in Paradise, Heroes of Red Hook* and *World War Cthulhu.* His work has earned several honorable mentions in *The Year's Best Fantasy and Horror* collections.

An entertainment columnist with Tampa Bay Newspapers, Lee has penned hundreds of film, theater and book reviews and has interviewed novelists as well as music industry icons such as Paddy Moloney of The Chieftains and Alan Parsons. His work for TBN has been recognized repeatedly by the Florida Press Association, including a first-place award for criticism in the 2013 Better Weekly Newspaper Contest.

Lee lives on the west coast of Florida with his wife and daughter. Visit www.leeclarkzumpe.com.

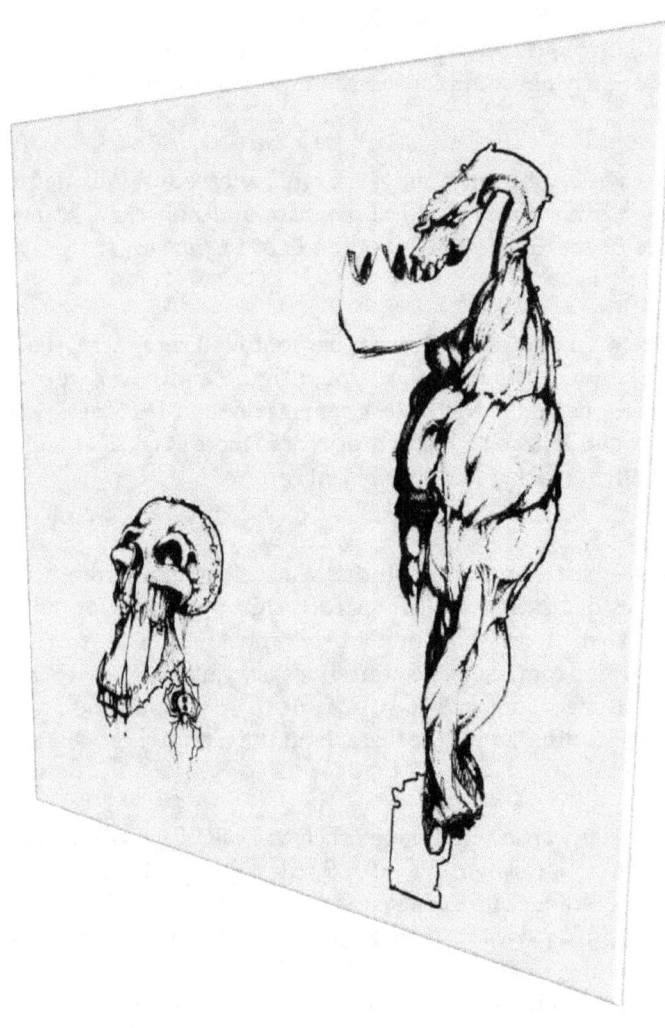